# COUNTDOWN OF A KILLA

## CLOCK'S TICKING

## LO-LIFE

LOCK DOWN PUBLICATIONS AND CA$H PRESENTS

Lock Down Publications

P.O. Box 944

Stockbridge, GA 30281

www.lockdownpublications.com

Like our page on Facebook: Lock Down Publications

www.facebook.com/lockdownpublications.ldp

# STAY CONNECTED WITH US!

Text **LOCKDOWN** to 22828 to stay up-to-date with new releases, sneak peaks, contests and more…

Like our page on Facebook:
Lock Down Publications

Join Lock Down Publications/The New Era Reading Group

Visit our website:
www.lockdownpublications.com

Follow us on Instagram:
Lock Down Publications

Email Us: We want to hear from you!

# DEDICATION

*Okay. Okay. Okay. Here we go again. Many of y'all probably didn't think we would make it this far. Well, I'm happy to prove y'all wrong. It seems that, no matter how many people I thank, I always remember that I forgot somebody. LOL.*

*Of Course. The Most High. If I wasn't in the position, I'm in, I would have never stumbled upon my gift. My passion for music, translated to a passion for writing books. So, thank you for that. To my beautiful mother and her twin sister. Y'all are the two single most influential people in my life. To my sister and strongest General, Tina Rene. Thank you for the long nights taking the time out to read each word I splash on these sheets and for having enough respect and courage to tell me if you don't like something. I value your opinion. Maybe you should write your own book one day. The rest of the fam. I do this not only for myself, but for y'all also. The goal is always the same. Only the method and means may change.*

*To all the little people, that made a big impact. Bay Bay (Waco stand up). To his sister Iesha: Stay on him, don't let him make it. Sometimes tough love is the only love you need. The original One Trey Seven. Lil Turk, D-Will, JD, Lil Ron, Lil Harvey, Fitzroy, Donte, Killa King, Bizzy Bee, Baby D, King Boobie, Kastro, Lil Ryan, D-Bo. Shout out to Oshay, Philly G, H-Town Gotty (Pleasentville stand up), my Saint Lucian Bredren, GoDj Hefna. You're doing it on a level, most can only dream of. Lil Twin (Charles Junior), Swisha, Juice, Aloe. I already gave these guys a shout out, but once isn't enough: Champ (Damn Fool, 5th ward, 5300 stand up.) A-1 (Antoine Benson, 5th Ward, 5300 stand up), Khamp (Marlo), Lucky 400, Boobie (Northwood, Baytown.) Happy (Cleveland Texas). Boo (Clinton Park, stand up). Pusha (Clinton Park, stand up). RIP to my niggas: Reggie aka Big Kaddy and Lil Gene Scott. (Too Playa) Shout out to Pablo Davis, Trinity Houston and his brother TK, Albert Hurd and AB (Big Big Homies.)*

*Now for the Ladies: Krystina Simmons, Jasmone Young, Aia Miller, LaKiesha Freeman, Ebone Gordon. Alexis Barnett, Ciera Senett, Jeanette Collins, Cierra Brinker, Rebecca Paulus, Sarah Mann, Brittany Riley, Raynisha Smith, Tajuna Williams. Dee and her niece Quinesha. Dominique Nash. Shout out to Jasmine A and Tanya B. Just know all y'all contributed to a nigga's life. Whether positively or negatively.*

*This is my third installment, and we've just begun. A lot of people want to know, where do I come up with the things I write about. The list of people above, can vouch for this. I'm as authentic as they come. It only makes sense that my work, can say the same.*

*To my wife Tracie Lamb. When you first took the leap with me, everyone doubted. Now, they see. I will always love you. Your loyalty is true and you've given me reason to fight even harder. I hope I've done the same for you.*
*To the rest, East up till my feet up. Bombs over Baggdad. They do it big, but we do it LARGE!*

# PROLOGUE

SHATYRA CHANEL JACKSON was the epitome of a bad bitch! At thirty-four years old, her 5'5", one hundred and forty pounds frame held her double-d breasts and forty-inch ass nicely. Her copper red skin tone complimented her honey glazed eyes. Growing up, she never had a problem snatching a man. Even if he belonged to someone else.

Shatyra, or Ty for short, had her first child at eighteen. She named the beautiful girl after her favorite R&B singer, Mya. Ten years later, Shatyra had a son, whom she named after his father, Chadwick Bowman Sr.

Chadwick Bowman, better known as Chad Bo, or just plain ole Bo, was a street nigga in every sense. Standing at five-foot-ten and weighing two hundred and five pounds, Bo had a reputation in the streets as a knockout artist. But make no mistake, he'd let his gun bark if need be.

Ty and Bo had been messing around since they were in high school. Bo caught an assault case when they were both eighteen. Two months after being booked in, he found out

Ty was pregnant with their first child. While incarcerated, Bo picked up welding skills, among other trades. He returned home to their newborn daughter, Mya.

Since his release, Bo lived a double life. While working as a welder, he sold exotic weed on the side. He was able to provide a decent living for his family. Even though life wasn't perfect, it was good.

"Oooh fuuccckk, baby. Damn, this dick feels soooo good!" Ty moaned. Her legs cocked wide open. Her pussy sucked on his dick. Her cat was so wet, it began to fart. Taking him hard and deep, 'Squish! Squish! Squish!' was all you heard. Ty begged him to fuck her harder. "Fuck this pussy, baby. Make me cum all on that big ass dick," she urged as he continued to pound into her wetness.

She gripped on his ass cheeks, pulling him in with each stroke, forcing him to go even deeper and deeper. Her orgasm began to build. She heard him call her "a nasty ass slut", and she lost it. "Aghhh ssshhit. I'm cummmmi- innnngg," she howled.

Ty's pussy exploded. Her cum skeeted, drenching his pubic hairs, down to his balls. As soon as he felt her release, he grunted, croaked and cried out. "Aghh fuck! Damn, bitch. This pussy wet than a motherfucka! I'm finna cummmm!" Even though he'd nutted in her countless times, he wanted to paint her face. He pulled out and strad- dled her chest. "Open up," he growled. She obeyed.

He jacked his cum-coated cock, unleashing spurts of warm cum all over Ty's face. Like a true porn star, she moaned and purred as he left her drenched and sticky.

Fully exhausted, he collapsed next to her. Ty, too tired to get up and clean herself, laid there. Although she was falling asleep, she heard him ask, "Where the keys at? I need to run to the store real quick." Instead of lifting her head up to respond, Ty simply pointed to her purse. He opened it up. She had about sixty dollars sticking out one of the side pockets. He snatched that, along with the keys and left her a cum-soaked mess. Seconds later, he was walking out the door.

As he pulled up to Circle A, he spotted a known dope fiend by the name of Paul, panhandling as usual. Paul still owed him one hundred dollars for an eight ball of hard he'd fronted him two weeks ago. He snatched a Houston Texans snapback from the backseat, put it on, and hopped out the Malibu.

Bo walked into the store, electing to deal with Paul after he got what he needed. Once he purchased the items, he headed back outside. Paul was lethargically walking towards the back of the building. Something told him to leave well enough alone, but his pride got the better of him. "Say. Look out, Paul!"

Paul turned around. His eyes grew big as saucers. Recognition set in. "Come here. I need to holla at you real quick," Bo said. Paul took off running. Obviously, he did remember he'd owed money.

Bo gave chase, catching up to Paul in no time. He swept Paul's legs from underneath him, causing Paul to tumble forwards. Before Bo realized what he was doing, Paul laid lifeless. He continued to kick and stomp on his head. Blood seeped from Paul's eyes and ears. His brain swelled. His heart stopped.

Once his fury and rage were sated, he quickly realized what he'd done. Panic seized him. He rushed back towards the front of the store, scooped up his items and hopped back in the Malibu. His heart beat rapidly as he contemplated his next move. Even though he didn't check Paul's vitals, he knew for certain he was dead.

He pulled back up to his apartment complex and wondered if he should tell Ty or not. He decided not to. He didn't need her running her mouth, getting him jammed up.

As he walked into the bedroom, he immediately took notice of Ty. She must have finally gotten herself up and cleaned the cum off her face. She laid asleep on her stomach. Legs spread wide. Pussy lips still swollen, glistening with residue.

He quickly got undressed, jacked his dick until it was primed and ready, then crawled between her legs and slid his eight-inch dick deep within her snatch. Ty moaned heavily, as they picked up right where they left off at.

---

**One Week Later**:

Bo was parked in Thorntree Apartments, his seat pushed all the way back. She was sucking the skin off his dick. "Ssshhiitttt, girl . . . Eat that dick up," he hissed as she pulled at his cock with her pillowy lips. '*Ghlup. Ghlup. Ghlup.*' Her head bobbed up and down. Her spit coated the sides of his shaft, dripping down to his nut sack.

He palmed the back of her head, interlocking his fingers

into her lace front. He began to pump into her mouth with more vigor. '*Ghlup. Ghlup. Ghlup.*' She struggled for air.

Bo watched as an older black woman came out of her apartment. She was dressed in a grey business suit, but he could tell she had a nice little bubble butt. Bo pictured her bent over, his dick sawing in and out of her asshole. His nuts began to boil. A thin layer of sweat began to form on his balls. He gripped her head tightly and announced his arrival. "Ssshit! I'm finna nut. Fuck! Aggghh."

His back jerked. Cum shot straight down her throat, coating her trachea. She gulped him down effortlessly, moaning around his dick as she squeezed and pulled out the rest of his baby batter.

Bo shivered and trembled. His dick head was too sensitive to continue. He grabbed her by her mane and pulled her off his rod.

Meme smacked her lips and giggled. She relished in another job well done. "Damn, Meme. Whoever taught you how to suck dick needs an award. You got the best head a nigga ever had."

"Boy, you ain't gotta tell me. A bitch knows her shit's pressure. I learned watching my momma suck dick," she confessed. Bo didn't even want to know what she meant by that. If he ever sees his momma sucking dick, he'd lose his marbles.

"When you gone come through, so a bitch can get some of that good ole dope dick?" Even though Bo loved the feel of Meme's wet pussy and her A-1 head, he knew he was playing a dangerous game. That's why he was reluctant to lead her on.

Meme was a bad bitch in her own right. At 5'4", yellow

bone, with full pink lips, perky C-cup titties and an ass like the Florida rapper, Jackie-O, Meme had her share of well-respected D Boys chasing after her. She was also, coincidentally, Ty's best friend. Or so Ty thought. "I'll try and swang back through tomorrow. During my lunch break," Bo said as he turned on the ignition. That was the sign prompting her to leave.

As she reached for the door handle, she looked back and said, "Imma hold you to that too, nigga." Meme stepped out of the passenger seat. Bo watched her walk away, her booty cheeks jiggling. Her ass crack swallowed up the cotton material. Even from the back, Bo could see a large wet spot. It seemed as if her asshole was wet. Bo wouldn't have been surprised, if Meme came while giving him head. What was ironic was that Bo had been messing with Meme almost as long as he'd been together with Ty.

Back when they were in high school, Ty had brought Meme with her to a kickback Bo and his friends were having. Ty had gotten sloppy drunk, as usual. Bo and a few of his friends carried Ty into the bedroom, where they tucked her in for the night.

While Ty was in bed, snoring, Bo was fucking Meme from the back. Two of his homeboys watched, waiting for their turn. Even though he loved Ty, Meme let him do what he wanted to her body. Nothing was taboo. Bo often brought other people into their bed. Once, for his birthday, he brought home two strippers. They spent the night fucking each other's brains out. Meme ate ass, and she just loved to suck dick. Ty was his lady in the streets, but Meme was his boss freak in the sheets.

Bo watched her walk into the apartment. He shook his

head. He knew he needed to leave her alone. Their relationship was wrong on so many levels. But he also knew he was going to be right back over there. Her pussy was just too good to let go, and her head game was the best he'd ever had.

He put the car in drive and made a right turn out of the apartment complex. Two dark colored sedans appeared out of nowhere, blocking him in. Bo instinctively reached for his pistol, until he noticed the blue and red police lights flashing. "What the fuck?" he said out loud, as he watched the sedan's doors open up.

Guns drawn and pointed at him, Bo was snatched out of the Malibu and placed in handcuffs. "Chadwick Bowman. You're under arrest for the murder of Paul Single. You have the right to remain silent. Any . . ." Bo was utterly confused. He had no clue who this Paul guy was, but he definitely knew he didn't kill him. After the detectives roughed him up, they threw him in the back of the car and took him downtown for booking.

# 1

TY BLEW out the potent smoke. Her whole body began to tingle as the THC traveled through her blood stream. Reruns of *Maury* played on the TV screen as she gripped and massaged Corey's hefty-sized dick with her right hand. Blunt in her left.

She looked at the door handle to make sure it was locked. The kids were playing in the living room. She didn't need them walking in and catching their momma with a mouth full of dick.

Corey was her boo thing she fucked on the side. She loved her baby daddy and the dick was good, but Corey brought out another side of her. Bo had been working so much lately. It felt as if he never had the time to tend to her needs. She knew it was fucked up to penalize a man for going to work to provide for his family, but Ty was a freak who needed sexual stimulation daily.

It wasn't like she was out there fucking every Tom, Dick and Harry. Besides Corey, her baby daddy was the only one that could say he felt what her pussy, mouth and ass felt like. Normally, she would have *never* brought Corey to the house, but Bo had gotten locked up and was currently in the county jail. She didn't see why she should leave the house just to get some good dick.

Ty hit the blunt one more time before she passed it back to him. She leaned over and placed him back into her mouth. "Mmmmh," she moaned as his dick slid over her taste buds. Corey's dick always tasted delicious to her. It had a hint of cinnamon and when he nutted, it was always sweet. With a pinch of salt.

She slid her hand between her thighs and felt how soaked and saturated she was. She had a fetish for sucking dick, and loved for a man to fuck her mouth until her throat became hoarse. His precum smeared over her tongue. To draw his cum from his balls became her obsession. Cardi B's *"Bodak Yellow"* played on the phone, while she bobbed up and down on his cock.

Ty contemplated letting it go to voicemail, but she knew it was Bo calling. Knowing him, he would blow it up until she answered. Might as well get it out of the way. "You have a collect call from . . ." She let Corey's dick fall out of her mouth before she sat up and pressed "zero" to accept.

Corey looked at her inquisitively. She held up a finger. *Wait a second.* He grabbed his dick and slowly jacked himself off. To keep himself ready while he sat and waited. "Hello?"

"What's up, Ty? You coming up here today?"

"Yeah, I'll be up there. I was going to take the kids to go see my momma, but if you want, I'll bring them too."

"Yeah. Go ahead and bring them through." Ty grabbed ahold of Corey's dick. Stroking it while she talked to Bo. "Did you talk to the lawyer?"

"I keep calling but he's never there. Plus, he never returns my calls." Ty dipped her head back down and took Corey deep into her mouth.

"That's bullshit. They gave me a hoe ass court-appointed lawyer. I already know that nigga ain't gone be talking 'bout doing shit for a nigga."

Ty pulled Corey's dick out so she could respond. "What is he telling you?" She stuffed Corey back in. This time, he grabbed her by her weave. Humping his hips, while her baby daddy tried to explain what his lawyer was saying.

"What time you coming up here?" Bo asked. Ty tried to pull off the dick so she could answer, but Corey wouldn't allow it. He held her head down, forcing her to finish what she started.

"Ty?...Ty?...You still there?" She struggled until she was finally able to break free.

"Yeah, baby...I'm here. The phone fell. I'll be up there around eight tonight." Corey got tired of the games. He stood up and positioned himself between her legs.

"Where the kids at?" Bo asked.

Even though they were in the living room, there was no way she was about to stop what she was doing to go get them. So, she lied. "They're outside playing, but we'll be up there tonight for sure," she said as Corey slid between her folds. She bit her bottom lip, to prevent herself from crying out as he touched the bottom of her pussy.

"That's a bet then. I love you."

"I love too," she moaned as she hung up, hoping he

didn't catch it. "Fuuuckkk Corey. You're a foul ass nigga," she cried as he worked his hips, digging in her twat.

"Yeah, whateva. You know you love that shit. Now shut your ass up and take this dick," he ordered. He placed her legs over his shoulders and gave her what she craved. After fucking her into a stupor, he got dressed, ready to leave. He smacked her on her ass and watched it jiggle. She peeled her eyes open. "I'm 'bout to bounce...You got some bread on you?"

Exhausted, Ty responded. "Not really. I got one hundred dollars, but that's for Bo. Imma put it on his books when I go see him later today."

Corey smirked to himself. "Look. I need to borrow it. I'll give it back to you tomorrow. You can put it on his books then."

Ty looked skeptical. "I already told him I was gonna put it on there tonight."

"Just tell him you had to do something for the kids. I'll make sure you have it by tomorrow," he claimed. She reluctantly gave in. After handing over the money, she had a feeling she'd never see it again. Which she never did.

---

"Girl, you going tonight or what?" Ty wanted to know.

"You still talking 'bout hitting that kickback?"

"Hell yeah. I went to see Bo the other day. That nigga has me stressed the fuck out. Plus, I haven't figured out what Imma do 'bout the bills. I need some time to let my hair down." Ty stood in the mirror admiring her figure. At thirty-four years old, she could give young bitches a run for their money.

"Momma, can we have some ice cream," little CJ pleaded.

"Girl. Hold on a second." Ty reached in her purse and grabbed four single bills. "Here, give it to your sister and tell her to buy some ice cream for y'all...Okay?"

"Yes, ma'am," he responded before scurrying off to go find his big sister.

"Hello?"

"I'm still here."

"Bitch. That boy looks just like his daddy."

"Shit, he looks more like you to me," Meme countered. Ty turned in the mirror to get a good look at her booty.

"Naw, Mya's fast ass looks *just* like me. Oh . . . I don't even tell you, girl. Her principal called talking 'bout they caught Mya trynna go into the boys restroom with some lil nappy head lil boy."

"Bitch. Shut up! When was this?"

"Two days ago. The teacher caught their asses, right before the act. Makes me wonder, how many times has she done it and not gotten caught. I asked her 'bout it. Guess what that silly lil bitch had to say."

"What?"

"She talking 'bout . . . *He just wanted to talk*."

Meme snorted a laugh. "Girl, I know she ain't hit you with *that*."

"Hmph! Either she fucking, or her ass is naive as hell," Ty admitted.

"Shit, bitch. No lie, *we* were fucking around that age.

Well, I was. You ain't start until your sixteenth birthday. By then, I was already taking dick in all three holes."

"Yeah. Your nasty ass is the reason I said fuck it, and let Tobias get up in them guts," Ty reminded her.

"Oh yeah. I forgot all about Tobias' ass." They kept on with the conversation until Meme claimed she had to take an incoming call. Ty tried to call Corey but he didn't answer.

She decided to get some fresh air. She threw on some black tights, a white tank top with some black and white flip flops. As soon as she stepped out of the apartment, she saw her kids playing by the pool. She couldn't help but feel sad. She honestly didn't know what the future held for them.

Bo kept telling her he was innocent. She wanted to believe him but why would they charge him if he didn't do it? She felt like he was just telling her that so she wouldn't leave him

What she did know though, was the bills were piling up. She had about six hundred dollars left in their savings. The only thing she could count on was the fact the Malibu was paid for. It was in Bo's name, but it was hers to do what she needed with.

She took off walking. No destination in mind. As she neared the laundromat, she saw two young niggas posted up. Smoking. Ty was low on cash, but she knew a pretty face and fat ass can get a bitch high, if nothing else. She headed in their direction. "Damn, momma. What's your name?" the darker one asked. The lighter one hit the blunt.

"Hold up, boy. How do I know you ain't no serial killer," she teased. "What's *your* name?"

"No offense, momma, I ain't mean nothing by it. This my nigga, Chubbs. And they call me Shooter," the darker one told her. "You smoke?"

Ty smirked. She liked the two young niggas. Especially the darker one. "What y'all smoking on? 'Cause a bitch ain't fucking with no reggie."

"Huh? Reggie? Momma, we don't do nothin' but smoke that Loud. This that Za Za right here." He passed her the blunt. Ty hit it twice. Her whole body began to tingle. Her clit started humming. She wet her lips. A warm sensation took over her body. Both of the young cats were trying not to stare at her camel toe. Their hungry stares had her feeling some type of way.

She rubbed her thighs together. "Uhmm...I gotta go," she whispered. More to herself, than them.

"Damn. Why you leaving so soon. We got some more smoke to blow. Plus, a nigga got some drank in the spot if you trynna get lit," Shooter offered.

Ty thought about it. She yearned to let loose. Throw caution to the wind. She desperately needed release, but her more rational mind was leading her away. Chubbs saw her indecisiveness and offered her a proposition. "How 'bout we pay you for your time?"

She looked at him with astonishment. She couldn't believe he just offered her money in exchange for some pussy. In all thirty-four years of living, never had Ty sold herself. She had sex with more than her fair share of men, but tricking had never been an option. "I don't know what you thought this was, but that ain't this." With that, she turned around and walked away, leaving the two young niggas staring at her backside.

She returned home and found the kids waiting on her. "Momma, can you fix us something to eat?" CJ asked as she led them inside.

"I got y'all. Go ahead and take y'all a bath, then come get something to eat." She looked in her purse. She only had twenty dollars on her. She exhaled before picking up her phone and ordering a pizza. As she waited for it to arrive, she couldn't help but think about the proposition Chubbs and Shooter offered her earlier. Could she ever do it? Sell her body for money? If so, then how much? As her kids stumbled back into the living room, the pizza arrived. Ty shook the thought of the indecent proposal from her head. Instead, she stood back and watched her kids have a meal. At least, for the night.

———

"Aye, girl, we got a problem."

"Aww shit. What's wrong now?"

"I can't find no one to watch my kids," Ty complained. "Lakiesha ass called, talking 'bout she had a date. And you know my momma can't be trusted. Plus, she gone want a bitch to pay her so she could go buy her some dope?"

"Okay. So what you gone do?"

"Shit. Imma leave their asses here. Mya's old enough to watch over CJ."

"I know that's right. What you wearing tonight?"

"Girl, I don't even know yet. I got this lil piece Bo bought me for my last birthday. I'll probably throw that on, with some Bottega heels. What *you* talking 'bout throwing on?"

"I ain't decided yet," Meme admitted. "Whateva it is, best believe I'ma try and shut that bitch down." Both women laughed it up, as they prepared to get dressed.

As Ty was getting dressed, she stood in the mirror, staring at the tattoo of Bo's name above her left titty. They'd been rocking with each other for close to twenty years. Through all the ups and downs, the cheating on both ends, they stuck together. Bo swore to her that he didn't do what they said he did. He told her to trust in the system.

She was honestly scared to picture a life without him. He was the reason she never had to get a job. He'd always been her provider. Her protector. Her *better* half. Her phone rang, disturbing her most intimate thoughts. "Hello?"

"What's up, baby?"

"Getting ready right now," Ty responded.

"What time you gone pull up?"

"Well, I'm a go scoop Meme around nine-thirty. So, I'ma say no later than ten."

"Bet that! You gone get lit?"

"Of course," she answered. "I need to take my mind off some shit."

"You know I got you, baby." Ty and Corey had an understanding. Neither one was looking for a commitment. Both were involved with other people. Ty had been fucking Corey on and off for about thirteen years. She cared deeply for Corey, but her heart belonged to Bo.

Once she was dressed, she triple checked herself in the mirror to make sure everything was in place. "Kids. Come lock the bottom lock," she yelled as she stepped out the door. She jumped in her Malibu and headed to go scoop up Meme.

Meme came out of her apartment, rocking a red Bebe skirt with a matching top. Some four-inch heels and some rose colored Cavalli shades. As she entered the car, Ty caught a light whiff of bubble gum. "So, who all spose to be there tonight?" Meme asked.

"A bunch of Corey's patnas. And some miscellaneous hoes from the West."

"I hope it's some niggas with a whole lot of money in that motherfucker," Meme sang. They both laughed, as Ty drove them to their destination.

Thirty minutes later, they pulled up to a two-story house in Alief. The party was packed, and Ty had a hard time finding a place to park. Corey told her it would be just a couple of his homies and some females. From the looks of it, this was a full-blown bash.

Loud music blared from the home stereo system as they approached the front door. As they entered, Ty texted Corey to see where he was at. He texted back. *Meet me in da backyard.*

"Hey, baby," he said as he hugged her, making sure to grip two handfuls of her ass. Ty moaned into the side of his neck. Corey raised the helm of her dress up, exposing her ass cheeks.

"Boy. What you doing?" She smacked him on the chest. "You know I ain't got no panties on."

"A'ight. Keep playing. You gone make a nigga buss this pussy open in front of everybody," he warned her.

"Yeah, whateva, nigga," she replied, clearly not believing his threat.

"You want something to drink?"

"Hell yeah. What y'all serving?" Ty needed to travel outside her body.

"Shit. We got damn near the whole store in this bitch," Corey informed her.

"Well, surprise me. You know what I like." With that, Corey took off to get her a drink. Meme had disappeared the minute she stepped foot in the house.

"Damn, girl. A nigga was just about to bounce, till I saw *you* come in. Now, I got a reason to stay. If you don't mind, what's your name, pretty lady?" A fine, chocolate specimen of a man approached her. Ty couldn't deny it. He was fine, with a capital F. 6'3" chiseled frame, and when she took a sneak peak at the front of his denim shorts, a very nice size bulge.

Her kitty purred. She needed to tame it quickly. "My name is Ty. Nice to meet you, but I'm here with Corey," she told him.

"Well, my name is Bryce. If you're ever in need of someone to talk to, I'll be here all night, waiting on you." He hit her with a seductive smile, before leaving her standing on the back patio, waiting for Corey to return. Moments later, Corey emerged with her drink.

After the first drink, she already felt torn down. He began to kiss on her neck. Sliding his hands underneath the helm of her dress. Caressing her slit, pushing his middle finger into her tight, wet hole. Even though they were surrounded by people, Corey had her so worked up, she didn't care. She jerked. A second digit plunged into her wetness.

Corey diddled her clit with his thumb as he finger-fucked her in front of everyone. "Oh my gawd...Baby, you finna make me cum...I'm finna cummm!" she cried out, while biting into his shoulder. Sticky cream coated his fingers.

Her orgasm subsided. Corey led her into the house and into an upstairs bedroom. He didn't bother to undress her. Instead, he pushed her forward and flipped her dress over her hips. He peeled her ass cheeks apart, while dropping his sweats. His dick flopped out. He rubbed it upon and down her slit, then rammed all eight inches into her cunt. Ty groaned, balled her fist up as she gripped the bedsheets. Corey fucked her into a dick-induced coma.

Ty awoke with a splitting headache. She found herself ass naked in a bed, with a man on each side of her. She smelled cum on her breath. Her asshole felt dilated. *What the fuck?* she thought as she stumbled out of bed. She searched for her phone and found it underneath a pair of boxers. The clock read 4:39 a.m.

She threw on her dress, then wandered off to go search for Meme or Corey. The party had died all the way down. Except for a few stragglers, there was no one left in the house.

Ty traveled from room to room in search of her best friend. She ended up walking in on Meme squatting over Corey. He held her up by her thighs, fucking the living daylights out of her. Ty watched as his balls swung wildly. Smacking Meme on the ass, as her pussy lips swallowed his dick. White froth coated his shaft. "Oh fuck. Oh fuck. Oh fuck. Corey...Damn, nigga, this dick feels sooo good!" Meme cried out as he fucked her with a vengeance.

Ty couldn't believe it. *Her best friend?* "This how the fuck y'all do me?" she screamed, startling the two. Before

Meme could react, Ty ran over and cold-clocked her in the side of the head, dropping her like a sack of potatoes. Meme fell off the side of the bed, crashing onto the floor. Unconscious.

Corey scooted up the bed, until his back was flush against the headboard. Dick sticking straight up. Still wet and glistening. Ty snatched a lamp out of the wall socket, and threw it at his head. "You nasty, bitch ass nigga," she seethed.

He rolled out of bed with his hands in the air. "Ty. Chill, my nigga. What you tripping on? It ain't like we're together."

"Yeah, but that's my best friend."

"Okay, but damn. You just let two nigga double-team you. So what you tripping 'bout?"

"What? What the fuck is you talking 'bout?" Ty was perplexed. She was too angry to even let what he was saying register in her mind.

"Come on, Ty...You know what. Whateva, man! If me fucking Meme gone have you tripping, then we can go our separate ways."

"So what you saying? If I don't let you fuck my best friend, you not trynna fuck with me?" Corey didn't answer. To Ty, that was answer enough. "You know what, Corey? You ain't shit. Tell that bitch when she wakes up, to find her own ride home. And I don't want to hear from her ever again. She's dead to me!"

Ty spat on Meme, before turning around and heading out the door. Only when she made it to the car, did she allow herself to cry. Corey and Meme were truly the only two people she had in her life besides her children and Bo.

Then, on top of that, she didn't even know how to start to dissect how she ended up in bed with two strange men. Ty was 34, but felt as lost as a 16-year-old runaway. She drove home realizing she had some major soul searching to do.

As she parked her car, she saw Shooter escorting a Hispanic woman with the body of a stripper back to her vehicle. No doubt, they just got done having the time of their lives. Ty couldn't help but realize she went through what she went through, and didn't get paid a dime. She contemplated approaching Shooter and asking him to elaborate on the proposal, but was conscious about the state she was in.

Smelling like a gallon of cum was not the best way to approach *any* man. She called it a night, locked up her car and headed inside to her sleeping kids.

# 2

BO STOOD PATIENTLY AWAITING his name to be called for commissary. After the last name was called and the workers packed up and left the pod, Bo realized that once again, Ty had left him hanging. It wouldn't be so bad if the food was decent. Everything that came through that slot was unfit for human consumption. Then, if it was halfway decent, it wasn't enough to feed an 8- year-old child. Much less a grown man.

He was pissed, to say the least. Ever since he'd gotten locked up three weeks ago, he had yet to make store. He really wasn't tripping on food, but the hygiene was non negotiable. When he was out there in the world, he made sure Ty and the kids had everything they needed. Bo couldn't understand why she was doing him like this.

She would always swear to him that she would take care of it. When she didn't, she always had an excuse. "Say, hood...You need something?" a young cat from Bo's hood asked him, while he sat on his bunk fuming.

"Naw, lil homie, I'm good. I appreciate it though." Back in his younger days, if Bo didn't go to store, he'd pull up on somebody and take their bag. Of course, he'd give them the option. Fight. If they win, they get it back. If he wins, well...To the victor goes the spoils.

Now that he was in his 30's, he felt that type of savagery was beneath him. He smelled his armpits. He was beginning to get ripe. With no deodorant, he was forced to take multiple showers a day, in order to stay fresh. Bo desperately needed a way to generate some money.

He grabbed his washcloth, state soap, and hit the showers. His thoughts lingered on Ty, and wondered what she was doing. The last time they had sex popped into his mind. His dick began to twitch. He reached down, grabbed his heavy cock and began to stroke it lightly. With the water beating down the back of his neck, Bo began to pump his dick slowly.

Then he pictured the last time he hit Ty from the back. She'd been on the phone describing to Meme how good the dick was feeling to her. Little did she know, Meme had just gotten some of that same good ass dick herself, a couple hours before. While Ty was at home taking a nap.

Bo then started reminiscing about Meme. When Meme called Ty, and described to her how good her boo "Troy's" dick was. Bo was balls deep in her banana red peach. Before he knew it, his balls ached. His shaft began to harden. He placed his left hand against the wall and braced himself. His body jerked. His dick began to spit. "Fuck!" He growled and groaned, as nut splashed and flowed down the drain.

After washing up real good, Bo got out of the shower

and made his way back to his bunk. He applied some hygiene he borrowed from his homie, Stank. "New house!" Bo looked up and noticed what was obviously a flaming homosexual entering the pod.

Dude was 5'8", brown-skinned and maybe 160 pounds, soaking wet. His hair was long and slicked back. If that wasn't proof enough, he walked with his wrist bent and hips swaying. He stopped at the door, looked around for an empty bunk. Coincidentally, the only bunk open was the one next to Bo's.

Bo really didn't have anything against gays, but he loved pussy and couldn't understand the lifestyle himself. "Hey. My name's Brown Sugar. You don't mind if I bunk next to you, do you?"

Bo looked at the open bunk, then back at Brown Sugar. "Shit, I don't own none of this shit. You can sleep where you want to." Brown Sugar eyed Bo for a second, admiring his chest and arms before he began to fix his bunk. Bo finished his hygiene and headed to Stank's bunk to return it. He then made his way to the day room to watch "The Voice".

He passed up a group of spade players gambling for soups. Bo was an exceptional spade player, but with no soups, he wasn't about to gamble on his ass. He was from the old school. A person could get their shit split open for gambling with no money to back up their bets.

As he stood watching the game, he heard that same soft feminine voice. "Do you play?"

"Huh?"

"Do you play spades?" Brown Sugar stood next to him, motioning towards the spade table.

"Yeah, but I ain't got no bread right now," he told him honestly.

"Are you any good?"

"Good? I'm the rawest thing on the pod. Maybe even the floor."

"Confident! I like that. Well, I'm pretty damn good myself, so I don't see why we should ever lose."

"Naw, I'm good. Like I said, I ain't got no money."

"Don't worry 'bout that. I'ma put you up. I don't miss no store. Plus, if I need money wired somewhere, it'll get sent. No hesitation."

Bo thought for a second. He shrugged. "Fuck it!" Him and Brown Sugar sat down at the table. For the rest of the night, their team never lost a game. When the DO's came in and announced it was rack time, Bo had fifteen soups, three bags of chips and two honeybuns.

He traded a few items for some hygiene. A deodorant and a toothpaste. He also bought a bar of Zest soap. Brown Sugar wasn't tripping. He allowed Bo to keep all his winnings as well. All he took was the initial bet. 2 soups.

As Bo sat back in his bunk, he couldn't believe his luck. Just that morning, he didn't have a soup to his name or any hygiene to speak of. Now, he had enough to last at least a week, maybe two. "Where you from, Bo?" Brown Sugar asked while laying on his side. Forearm folded under his face.

"I'm from the East. Uvalde. Oaks of Woodforest. Where you from?"

"I'm from the West, but I be everywhere. Matter fact, I was just on Uvalde two weeks ago. They had a birthday bash for my nephew at Mr. Gatty's," Sugar told him.

"Gatty's? I know where that's at...What you do? Why they lock you up?" Bo couldn't picture the little, frail dude committing any crimes.

Brown Sugar tried to decide if he should divulge the details of his case. He took a deep breath. "Well. They say I *allegedly* stabbed someone." Bo raised his eyebrows.

"You? Stabbed somebody?" Bo couldn't hide his skepticism.

"Don't look so surprised. I'm small. If I gotta to get active, then I gotta pick something up."

"I can feel that," Bo responded.

"Sooo. What they say *you* did?"

"They talkin 'bout I killed someone. A person I've never met," Bo claimed. It was Brown Sugar's turn to look skeptical.

"You sure you've never met him?"

"Of course I'm sure. Wouldn't you be if they claimed you murdered a person?" Bo said vehemently.

"You're right about that." Brown Sugar looked like he had something he was struggling to express. "Look, Bo, I have a proposition for you. I know this is jail and I'm small. Plus, I take that dick, so most of these guys look at me as prey. I see how they respect you and get out your way when you walk through. I'm willing to pay you every week to watch my back. Either I can give you some commissary, cash, or both.

Bo's head began to spin. He wasn't sure how that would look. Him protecting a punk in jail was the same as him sticking his dick up in one. At the same time, he knew what was really going on. No one was willing to help him survive. How could they hold the right to judge? He didn't know what was going on with Ty, but until she got her shit together, he had to do what he had to do.

After a few moments, Bo decided. "How much are we talking bout?"

"How 'bout $100 a week, until I leave?"

Bo couldn't believe it. He would have done it for $10 a week. In jail, $10 a week could cover his basic necessities. "That's a bet!" He was excited.

They continued to talk well into the night. For the first time since he'd been booked, Bo went to bed *without* thinking about Ty.

————

Marcus was a troubled young man from the start. Born to a mother who had meth in her system, Marcus was immediately taken from her and awarded to the State. With no family stepping up to claim him, Marcus grew up in foster care. In his 17 plus years of existence, he'd been through twenty different foster homes.

He had tremendous trouble in school and was classified as remedial. Even though he was slow of wit, he was strong as an ox. With a penchant for violence, he could become quite aggressive when upset. With no one to show him how to manage and taper his rage, Marcus would end up beating someone badly. Thus, getting kicked out of another home.

*Six months ago, he was living with a couple by the name of Joe and Betty. They were a white couple who could care less about the kids. To them, it was all about the state check.*

*Joe was a medium-sized man with a slight pouch. He*

*had beady eyes, and a thick coarse beard. Joe was an alcoholic who was rarely at home. When he was, he wouldn't hesitate to put his hands on someone. A lot of times, it would be Betty.*

*Betty was a woman in her early 40's, but carried it well. Dirty blond hair, crystal blue eyes. Big breasts with a wide, soft booty. Marcus used to always fantasize about Betty, wondering, how could a dude like Joe ever snatch a woman like her.*

*One night, while Joe was out drinking, rain started to pour down heavily. That particular home housed four teenage boys. Three of them had found a way to escape for the night, leaving Marcus at home alone with Ms. Betty.*

*Marcus was watching movies in his room when the lights went out. He grabbed his cell phone and used it as a light source, then sought out Betty. He found her in the garage, looking for the breaker box. After flipping the switch multiple times, she became frustrated. "Let me try," Marcus offered up.*

*She moved out of the way and stood behind him. It was so dark, they could only see about six inches in front of their faces. As Marcus began to work on the breaker box, he felt Ms. Betty's hands slide into the elastic waistband of his gym shorts.*

*He froze, unsure of what was going on. It was so quiet, he could hear his blood rushing through his veins. His heart thundered in his chest. "Ssshh, baby. Let momma get you right," she coo'd in his ear. Betty pulled out his overgrown 9-inch dick out. With her titties pressed against his back, she stroked him with her right hand. Her left massaged his abs. "Damn, boy. This black cock is so fucking big. Y'all always have such big cocks. You gone let momma taste it?"*

*Marcus couldn't answer verbally, but his dick jumped. Betty knew she had him. Unbeknownst to Marcus, Betty did this every so often. She would sit and observe, trying to decipher who would keep their mouth shut, as well as who had the best package. From what she gathered, she'd hit the jackpot. That night, Betty fucked and sucked young Marcus until he was depleted and exhausted. At least two to three times a week, they would hook up. Before long, Marcus was making her cum at will.*

*One night, Joe happened to get kicked out of the bar he frequented. Coming home early, only to find his wife of ten years, on her hands and knees. Getting stuffed with black cock up her tight little rosebud. Joe went ape shit, attacking Marcus. But Marcus honed his skills on the streets and playgrounds. Joe was left with a broken jaw and a shattered nose. Suffice to say, Marcus was kicked out of the home.*

Now, he was about to be eighteen years old in two weeks. He couldn't wait. The day was finally coming where he would be starting his brand new life on his own.

Marcus sat in the living room listening to Lil Durk on his Beats headphones. He noticed his phone light up. He grabbed it and answered. "What's up?"

"Damn, Marcus. You ain't hear me knocking on your window?" His best friend, Chief, stayed next door. Every morning he would wake Marcus up with a knock on his window.

"Naw, I had the headphones on. I'm 'bout to come out."

"You got some blunt wraps? I ran out last night." Marcus looked under his dresser and reached for his stash. After grabbing two blunt wraps, he threw on his Houston Astro's snapback and headed out the door.

The day Marcus moved in, him and Chief met, blew a blunt and remained the best of friends ever since. Chief, whose real name was Calvin, was a short, stout, brown-skinned kid. He loved to do what his nickname suggested. "Chief!"

He woke up smoking and went to bed smoking. Chief stayed at home with his mom: Laura, and his big sister— Cindy. Laura was a single mother, who had her first child when she was twenty-two and her second when she was twenty-four. Brown-skinned, with a nice juicy booty. Blessed with some perky B-cups, and a pair of full, pouty lips, Laura was definitely a Grade A MILF. Her daughter— Cindy—was a carbon copy. At the age of nineteen, she was on pace to become her mother's identical twin.

Marcus walked into the house. A pleasant aroma of cinnamon and jasmine invaded his nostrils. The kitchen was on the way to the Chief's room. As they passed it up, Marcus got a bird's eye view of Laura bending over, grabbing something out of the oven.

With a pair of Daisy Duke denim shorts on, Marcus could see one of her meaty sex lips hanging out the side of the crotch band. Her coochie was eating up the material. Her ass swayed as she hummed to an old R&B tune. Marcus was so hypnotized, he never saw the dining room chair. Until he collided with it.

Laura was startled. She looked back, saw Marcus and

smiled. "Hey, sweetie. I didn't know you was coming over."

"Oh yeah, Chief...I mean Calvin wanted me to come play *Call of Duty*." Marcus couldn't keep his eyes off her beasts. Her nipples were like tiny stones protruding through the thin material of her tank top. He felt his dick twitch. He couldn't help but lick his lips as he eyed her gigantic camel toe.

Laura wasn't lost on his reaction. On the contrary, she was flattered. Even though Marcus was young, he was built like a thirty-year-old man. Standing at six feet tall and weighing 215 pounds of solid muscle, his mere presence would leave her wet and wanton. "Well, I hope you can stay for lunch. I'm cooking fried fish, French fries, mac and cheese, as well as an upside down lemon 7Up cake."

Marcus' stomach began to growl. "Sure thing, Ms. Sage."

"Please. How many times I gotta to tell you? Call me Laura."

"Right. My bad, Laura."

"Now, that's better. Y'all boys go ahead. I'll call y'all when the food is ready. Shouldn't take long. Maybe about another hour." As the boys walked off, Laura took a good look at Marcus's ass. She pictured herself grabbing and holding onto his cheeks, as he fucked her mouth with his glorious dick until his cum filled her belly to the brim. She shivered at the thought.

Marcus entered Chief's room, only to discover he'd already twisted up a blunt and was preparing to light it. Marcus flopped down onto the red bean bag chair and grabbed his customary 2nd player controller. "What's in the deck?"

"*Call of Duty: Black Ops*. What else? What you trynna do?" Chief wanted to gamble.

"Shit. I don't have no bread right now," Marcus told him.

"Well, how 'bout this. I win, you go with me on the lick tonight. If you win, you call it."

"Lick? What lick you talkin' 'bout?"

Chief smirked. "Oh, I didn't tell you 'bout the lick?" Chief pulled on the blunt twice, before he passed it to Marcus and began his spiel. "Okay, look. My sister Cindy's been fucking with this wack ass D Boy by the name of Keon. The nigga be selling the type of shit we're smoking on right now. Straight gas! Two days ago, my sister said he got a new shipment. She said she overheard him say it was fifty elbows."

Marcus raised an eyebrow at the mention of Cindy giving up that type of info. Chief slightly shook his head and continued. "My sister ain't down with jacking the nigga. She was just bumping her gums. Flexing, but I know she'll be with the nigga out on the town tonight. I wanna break in his shit and peel his ass. We'll buss it down 50/50." Chief reached for the blunt back. "So wassup? You gone fuck with it or what?"

Marcus felt the THC travel through his veins. No doubt about it, the weed they were smoking was some of the best he'd ever smoked. He wasn't sure about breaking into dude's house, but he needed some money and some more smoke. Then, he wasn't about to leave his nigga out to dry. "Fuck it. I'll go," he agreed as he grabbed the blunt back.

About an hour later, Laura knocked on the door and asked them if they wanted her to bring them their plates. "Yes," they said in unison. She left to go get the food. Chief's phone rang. After seeing who it was, he answered but left the room to go talk in private.

Marcus sat back and thought about all the things he could do with that weed. He knew he couldn't smoke it all, but he'd never hustled, so he didn't know the first thing about selling it. Laura came back in the room with the two plates. She sat Chief's plate on his dresser. Marcus couldn't help but admire her body.

Her shorts were so tight, he could clearly see her pussy lips protruding. As she walked over to Marcus and stood before him, he caught a whiff of her scent. Laura's need was evident. Since he was sitting down and she was standing up, his face was eye level with her crotch. "Here you go, Mr. Marcus." She giggled at her inside joke, then bit her lower lip seductively.

His dick began to come alive. Thoughts of him sliding his tongue between her folds danced in his head. His mouth watered. He yearned to taste her juices. "Umm. Thank you, Ms. Laura."

"You're so very welcome, young man. Why don't you ever spend the night with Calvin?" Laura wanted him bad. She needed to make it as clear as possible.

"Um. I really don't know. I guess I just never thought about it."

"Well, I'll be going out tonight with a friend. I know Cindy has a date. So you and Calvin can have the house to yourselves. Until I get back, that is. Maybe you can keep an eye on him."

Marcus chuckled. I can always try, but um . . . sure, I'll spend the night."

Laura bit her lip again. Before she could respond, Chief popped back into the room. He saw Marcus with a plate. "Momma. Where's my plate?"

Instead of answering, she pointed to the dresser, turned around, and headed out the door, making sure her ass cheeks jiggled as she switched from right to left. Marcus didn't know what it was. Older women did it for him. Probably because most of his sexual experiences came from fucking his foster mothers.

"I got somebody that says they want ten of them things, once we get them," Chief spoke, breaking Marcus out of his erotic daydream.

"Huh? Say what?"

"The bows, my nigga. They said if we get them, they'll buy ten for $6,500. We can split that lick in half. You give him five and I'll give him five."

Marcus shrugged. "A'ight. Fuck it!" He had his mind on one thing at that time: tearing into the food. The boys ate while they discussed the lick. Chief suggested that Marcus spend the night. Of course Marcus agreed, neglecting to tell Chief that he'd already been invited by his mother.

# 3

Around 9:30 P.M., Laura got ready to go out on her date. She was dressed in an all-black, see-through silk Versace dress. Black heels and a black Gucci clutch. You could tell she was wearing a thong. Every step she took, her ass cheeks wobbled. Her perfume was intoxicating. Marcus had to constantly readjust himself. His dick was so hard that it ached. He had to lay it flat against his abs, to relieve the pressure.

"A'ight, boys. Y'all stay y'all asses out of trouble. I'll be back late tonight," she told them as she left out the door. Cindy left twenty minutes later. The boys got themselves ready.

"A'ight, check game. I turned the GPS locator on my sister's phone on. We'll be able to track her from the spot, to wherever they go. Once they get to where they're going, we'll make our move." Marcus nodded in understanding, but was still thinking about Laura. All that ass she had swayed.

Chief pulled up his phone and went to the GPS app. "They just left the spot. It looks like they're headed to the Southwest." Chief began to get dressed. Before they left, they each had on all-black, with black bandannas in their back pockets. Neither one of them had cars. They rode their bikes. Each sporting a black backpack.

They arrived in Woodforest North subdivision. Chief checked his phone. Keon and Cindy stopped at a restaurant called Chacho's. They stopped to eat. "We can go ahead and park the bikes on the side of the Vaco. Then, we'll hit the fence into the nigga backyard. He ain't got no dogs, or alarms. We should be good," Chief said.

Marcus realized something, then looked at him. "Wait a minute. Do we even know where the stash at?"

"Not really. I just know it's in the house fa sho, but we gone have to look around."

"What? Come on, man. You mean to tell me, you don't know where the stash is?"

"Man, chill. I know it's in there. How many places can you stash fifty pounds? Huh?"

Marcus shook his head, exasperated. "A'ight, man. Let's go. I hope that shit is in there. A nigga ain't trynna go through all this for nothing." They parked their bikes and hopped the fence of the house behind Keon's. Moments later, they were in *his* backyard.

They checked the patio door. It was locked. They checked each window. Finally, Lady Luck was on their side. The kitchen window happened to be unlocked. Since Marcus was taller, he helped Chief through the window first. Once Chief gained entry, he unlocked the patio door.

As soon as they entered, they split up. "I'll go upstairs,

and you cover downstairs," Chief told him. They searched everything and everywhere. Dresser drawers. Flipping couch cushions. Twenty minutes into the search, they still hadn't found what they were looking for.

Sweat poured from their pores. They began to get frantic. Time was against them. Chief checked the GPS. Cindy and Keon were on the move. Good news was, they weren't heading home. "Bro, we gotta to hurry up. Ain't no telling when they'll be coming back." The house looked like a tornado hit it.

Chief got to thinking. *Where haven't we looked yet?* He sat down and thought it out. Then it hit him. *The garage!* He took off with Marcus in pursuit. When they entered the garage, they searched and found a deep freezer with a lock on it. "Fuck," he yelled as he looked for something to break the lock.

They tossed things around, until Marcus found a hammer. He reared back and brought the hammer down with great force. After three tries, the lock broke off. Chief lifted the freezer door. They couldn't believe it. There, sitting in the freezer was fifty pounds of grade A marijuana. To some, fifty pounds of weed isn't much. But to a couple of teenage boys, fifty pounds might as well have been 50 kilos.

They rushed to stuff their backpacks full. Soon, they discovered they needed more space. Chief ran back into the kitchen and grabbed some black trash bags. They stuffed the rest of the weed into them. They grabbed the two pistols they found and the little bit of cash they came across, and they jetted.

After hopping fences like the 200 meter hurdles, they

were back at their bikes. Chief checked the GPS. It said that they were exiting Federal Road and would be back at the house in ten minutes. They tossed the bags over their shoulders and pedaled like their life depended on it.

Moments later, they were sitting in Chief's room, drenched in sweat, chest heaving, struggling to catch their breaths. "Damn, Chief. Where we spose to stash all this shit?"

"We gone put it in the attic right now. Tomorrow, we gone figure out what to do with it. We already got ten of them hoes sold, so . . ." Chief put everything they found in the attic before he hit the shower.

Marcus couldn't stop shaking. Not from fear, but from excitement. His whole life, he never had more than a couple hundred dollars at a time. And that's only when he was fortunate to have foster parents that packed fair. He knew this would be the lick that would help him get on his feet, when he was finally free of the system.

After Chief got out of the shower, Marcus went in. While he soaped up, he thought about Laura. Her scent. Her sexuality. The way the dress clung to her curves. He began to stroke himself. Fantasizing about how it would feel to bend her over and eat her ass from the back. His foster mother Rachel made him eat her ass one night. Ever since then, he'd been hooked on the act.

Once he squeezed one off and hopped out the shower, he immediately knew something was wrong. He heard hysterical crying and followed the sound until he came upon the source. There, in the living room was Cindy. Lip busted. Eye swollen shut. Chief stood over her, with his fist balled and his face mugged up. If looks could kill, Chief would have been a serial killer. "What's going on?"

Chief looked up and noticed Marcus draped in a bath towel, but neglected to say anything. "That bitch nigga put his hands on my sister. Talking 'bout he thinks she had something to do with his punk ass getting robbed."

"What! But Cindy's been fucking with dude for a minute." Upon hearing that, Cindy began to cry even louder.

"Whhyyy! Why did he do this to me? I would never do anything like that to him," she balled. Snot and blood bubbled and ran out her nose. Marcus felt fucked up. He and Chief were the reason Cindy got her ass whooped. She honestly didn't have anything to do with it. Chief gave him a knowing look. Marcus retreated back to Chief's room to get dressed.

When he emerged, Marcus could see death written all over his best friend's face. "This some bitch ass shit, bro. This nigga done got the nerve to put his hands on my sister." Tears trickled down Chief's face. He balled his fit, and punched through the wall. Marcus sat quietly, waiting on Chief to tire himself out.

Finally, he calmed down enough to have a civilized talk. "Bro, we can't let this nigga get away with this. Cindy ain't have shit to do with that nigga getting robbed."

Marcus nodded solemnly. "So, what you wanna do?" That was the million dollar question.

"We gone have to pull up on his ass," Chief said forcefully.

"And do what?"

"I don't know yet. But I'ma figure it out. Man, this shit

so fucked up. I'm 'bout to lay down, bro. We'll talk in the morning." Marcus prepared a pallet on the floor. He stripped down to his gym shorts and drifted to sleep.

Around 4:30 in the morning, Marcus dreamt someone sliding their hands into his gym shorts. Squeezing. Gripping his dick as they pulled him out and jacked him off slowly. He felt something hot and wet cover the helmet. A soft moan escaped his lips as he felt his balls being lightly sucked on. He opened his eyes. His best friend's mother was on her hands and knees, with his nine-inch dick lodged in her mouth.

She kissed the head twice, before licking up and down the sides of his shaft. "Ohh shit," Marcus groaned.

Laura put her fingers to his lips. "Shhh. We can't wake him up," she whispered. Chief was asleep on his bed just a few feet away. Marcus nodded his understanding as Laura began to give him some slow and methodical head. She allowed her saliva to coat his cock, while she bobbed her head with purpose. Pulling out his cum like a vacuum cleaner.

She popped him out of her mouth and ducked under to tackle his nut sack. Marcus squirmed and fidgeted, unable to properly express how good she was making him feel. Soft sucking sounds could be heard over the light snores Chief was making a mere five feet away.

Laura's left hand eased down to her box. Her middle finger glided through her sex lips, plucking at her engorged clit. She slipped two fingers into her sopping wet cunt and began to fuck herself feverishly.

Marcus gripped her head tightly, fucking her throat at the same fevered pace. Being the seasoned vet that she was,

Laura handled the dick like a pro, letting the young nigga have his way with her mouth. Marcus began to feel hot, his balls heavy. He looked at how her ass was tooted up, her head in his lap. He wondered how her pussy felt. Her womanly scent intoxicated the room. It was too much to bear.

While gritting his teeth and bucking his hips, Marcus gripped both sides of Laura's head and unloaded deep into her throat. His cock jumped, twitched and jerked. Laura swallowed load after load of his delicious baby batter.

She squeezed him at the base and pulled up. His dick popped out of her mouth. She whispered, "Hmm . . . Hmm . . . Hm. Boy, I knew you had some good tasting dick. If my kids weren't here, I'd fuck you into the ground." Marcus, clearly winded, could do nothing but smile. Laura kissed his dick head one more time, then tucked him back in before getting up and leaving the room.

He watched as her ass cheeks jiggled. Marcus could clearly see her pussy juices glimmer in the light as it trailed down her inner thigh. Laura was a super freak, and he knew before it was said and done, he had to get some more of her.

Three days later, after they finally sold the ten pounds, they sat in Chief's room smoking weed as they tried to figure out their next move. They couldn't just start advertising. The streets talk. The last thing they needed was for Keon to find out they had weed. Especially since he was already falsely accusing Cindy. They knew what they had to do, but they'd been avoiding the conversation.

Chief sat with his head down, while Marcus played on his phone. Suddenly, Chief had an epiphany. He snapped his head up. "I got it. I figured out what we should do about Keon. We can't keep putting it off. The nigga KP told me, Keon plans on snatching my sister up and making her tell him who she was supposedly working with. As you know, Cindy's been out of town at my uncle Claude's house in the country. She comes back tomorrow. Marcus. We can not let anything happen to her."

Chief's eyes became misty. The realization that he could be the cause of his sister's death, began to settle in. Marcus, feeling the gravity of the situation, put his phone down. "So. What's the plan?"

"We got to smoke the nigga. Ain't no other way." Marcus's heart dropped to his stomach. Robbery and burglary are one thing. But killing someone? He wasn't sure he could pull that off. At the same time, he was also part of the reason Cindy was being accused. He felt he had to do something to protect her.

"A'ight. I'm down," Marcus conceded, understanding that his life was about to change drastically. Chief went into the attic and retrieved the two guns they'd stolen from Keon's crib. Chief kept the Glock .40 and Marcus got the Taurus .45. The two of them sat in the room, desperately trying to come up with a way they could get the drop on Keon, but still get away scot-free. After an hour of planning, they felt they had a sufficient solution to their problem. Now, it was a matter of waiting for the right moment.

KP was Keon's cousin, through marriage. Still, he hated Keon with a passion. When Keon used to go to visit KP's family, he used to torture KP to no end. It got so bad, KP would shake and shiver at the mere mention of Keon's name.

As they got older, KP began to tighten up. Keon would no longer be able to pick on him, but KP never forgot some of the sadistic things that were done to him.

When his homie, Chief, reached out to him about the situation with Keon and his sister, KP was eager to help. They came up with a plan. KP knew Keon couldn't resist a good dice game. He decided he would throw one behind JB's corner store. The plan was for Chief and Marcus to come through and lay everybody down. Rob the dice game, then of course leave Keon dead.

As Marcus got ready to slide, he couldn't shake the feeling that something was off. He attributed it to the fact he never killed anyone. And maybe it was just jitters.

Midnight came. Chief received the text from KP, letting him know everything was in place. They both rode their bikes over to JB's and hopped off in the apartments across the street.

Once they secured their bikes, they made their way through the trees. They approached the group from the backside of the store. From the treeline, Chief could see four different people shooting dice. Even from that distance, they could tell Keon was the one with his back towards him.

Chief pulled out his phone and texted KP the "Go word". KP read it, then excused himself as if he needed to make an important call. *The signal.*

The two pulled their ski masks on, and methodically made their way out from the bushes. The whole time, the group was so immersed into the game, no one noticed the two masked men approaching until Keon got smacked in the head with the pistol. "Aggh shit. What the fuck?" Keon screamed in agony. '*Thwack . . . Thwack . . . Thwack.*' Chief continued to pistol-whip Keon until his face was a bloody mess. His jaw, plus two of his front teeth, were shattered.

Marcus held down the other gamblers at gunpoint, while Chief went in Keon's pockets. Keon held the wound in his head and begged them to spare his life. "Look, man . . . That's all I got. I don't know who you are, so you don't have any reason to kill me. Please man. I don't wanna die."

It amazed Marcus how Keon seemed like such a *G Type* nigga, but as he laid on the ground covered in his own blood, he screamed and begged as Cindy must have, when he was beating her ass.

Marcus told the other gamblers to empty out their pockets as well. Once he was satisfied they were all broke, he turned towards Chief. The moment of truth. Could they follow through with this. Chief adjusted his grip on the gun at least ten different times. Marcus could see Chief's hands trembling, chest heaving as he worked up the nerve to squeeze. "Please man . . . Don't kill me. Please!"

Keon continued to beg. Chief closed his eyes and pulled the trigger. '*Bocka. Bocka.*' One shot hit him square in the chest. The other clipped his shoulder, spinning him face down into the gravel. Both boys took off running.

Once they made it to the apartments, they took off their masks. They jumped on their bikes and pedaled like hell, trying to make it back home. By the time they made it, they were drenched in sweat, unable to catch their breath. Chief wiped the guns down and placed them back in the attic. After promising to meet up the next day, they separated.

After heading back to his foster home, Marcus laid back in bed and thought about everything that had transpired. He asked himself. *Could I ever pull the trigger? Could I take a life?* He thought about it so much, he went to bed dreaming about it.

The next morning he heard loud banging on his window. 'Boom! Boom! Boom!' *What the fuck?* Marcus got up and opened his bedroom window. Chief stood with a panicked look on his face. "Wassup, nigga?"

"Man . . . We fucked up. That nigga KP called me early this morning. That nigga Keon didn't die."

"What?"

"Bro. That nigga's in the hospital. That ain't the worst part. The bitch nigga knows it was me. He told KP he recognized my Lebrons. He was with my sister when she bought them for my birthday. These hoes are special editions. That's not even all of it."

Marcus looked at him with disbelief. "So there's more?"

"Man. KP says this nigga is talking to the laws. He overheard him telling the police who did it."

Marcus couldn't believe it. "That nigga told on you? I thought he was a gangsta!"

Chief shook his head. "Dawg. This shit is all the way fucked up."

"A'ight. Well, let me brush my teeth. Imma come over so we can figure out the next step."

"Bet," Chief said. He made his way back to his house. Marcus got himself together, threw on some clothes. By the time he made it outside, cops were everywhere. Marcus's heart dropped. He worried for not only Chief, but for himself. He stood frozen and witnessed the cops bringing out his best friend in handcuffs.

Laura screamed and begged to know what was going on. He and Chief locked eyes. Marcus instantly knew what needed to be done. He had to find a way to get inside the house, grab the guns and dope before the cops came back looking for it.

They threw Chief into the cop car. Laura hopped in hers and followed them down to the precinct. Marcus contemplated breaking into the house to grab the stuff, but thought of a better idea.

# 4

Iт's 7:30 a.m. Ty just got done making sure her kids caught the bus for school. Now, she was getting herself ready to go job hunting. They finally gave Bo a bond. At $300k, it was no way he would be able to make it. Plus, her bills were piling up. With no steady income, she desperately needed a job.

Dressed in a navy blue Micheal Kors business suit with some navy blue pumps, Ty could easily be mistaken for a lawyer or real estate agent. As she was leaving the apartment and locking her door, the manager seemed to appear out of nowhere. "Ms. Jackson. We need to have a talk."

The manager was an older black man, with a "George Jefferson" hairline and an "Uncle Phil" stomach. "Uhh. Mr. P, I really can't right now. I'm headed to a job interview."

"Well, it won't take long. You're behind on your rent like two months. Now, I've been very lenient with you because you have those two babies, and their father's locked up. Ms. Jackson. If you don't have your rent in two weeks, you'll be homeless." Ty froze in her place.

She wanted to beg him to give her more time. Implore him to think about her kids. She longed to tell him, she had nowhere else to go. But her pride wouldn't allow it. Instead, she simply responded. "Okay, Mr. P, I'll have your money." With that, she left him standing on the welcome mat. He was watching her ass move in her somewhat tight, business skirt.

Ty had an interview at a doctor's office. A secretarial position. After three minutes, they told her they would get in touch. Then, someone showed her to the door.

Now, she had nothing else to do, but drive around asking for applications. To say she was depressed was an understatement. Once she noticed her gas tank reach half way, she knew it was time to take it in.

She pulled up to her apartment complex.

She told herself it was strictly to get some smoke. But deep down inside, her curiosity had been piqued. She wanted to learn more about Chubbs and Shooter's proposition. She parked, and decided to walk around for a bit. She approached the same laundromat she'd seen them smoking in a couple weeks prior.

At first, she was going to just walk past. Something urged her to go in. What she saw nearly made her have a heart attack. There was her daughter Mya, standing between some dudes legs, while he sat on top of a washing machine. Ty couldn't believe what she saw.

Mya had both hands wrapped around dude's enormous dick, as she sucked and slurped for dear life. "What the

fuck!" Ty screamed. Both Mya and her date jumped, startled and embarrassed.

"Oh my God. Momma! What are you doing here?"

"Bitch. I know your ass ain't just asked me that. You
nasty lil hoe. You're supposed to be in school, but instead
you're in a laundromat sucking dick." Ty was livid.

Dude hopped off the washer, pulling up his boxers and
jeans. His big floppy dick hanging over his waistline. He
had to pull his pants back down so he could slip his cock
back in place. "And you! Motherfucker, how old are you?"

He threw up his hands as if he was talking to the police.
"I'm sorry, ma'am. I'm . . . I'm eighteen."

"Nigga, your ass is lying. Ain't no way you're eighteen
with all that dick. Let me find out you're over eighteen and
Imma have your dirty ass locked up." The boy ran out of
there as quickly as possible. Mya kept her head down.
"Mya. I can't believe you out here like this. Take your ass
in the house. You know I'm 'bout to beat the black off your
ass."

"Yes, ma'am." Mya began to cry as she attempted to
walk past her mother. 'Smack!' Ty slapped her across the
side of the face, causing her to crash into the soda
machine.

"Bitch. What you crying for? I'm 'bout to give your ass
something to cry about in just a lil bit." Mya held on to the
side of her face and ran all the way home.

Ty took a deep breath to calm her nerves. Her life was
falling apart before her very eyes. She jumped back in her
car and cried her eyes out. She never understood how much
she really needed Bo. Now that he was gone, she didn't

know what to do. She needed to figure something out. Quick, fast and in a hurry!

———

"New House!" The customary call was announced. Bo and Brown Sugar were once again running the spade table as usual. Since the inception of their partnership, Bo was sitting fat on commissary. Plus, his protection agreement with Brown Sugar had his account looking decent. In the months since, he'd been able to stack up close to two bands on his books. His spade game took care of his eating, so he didn't really need to go to store.

Bo took notice of the new house. He looked real familiar. Bo couldn't place the face with a name. After the new house placed his bedroll on the empty bunk, he went straight to the phones. Bo couldn't stop staring at him. He felt he knew him for certain.

Once the new house hopped on the phone and began to discuss his situation, it clicked. Now, Bo knew exactly where he knew him from. The new house ended his call, then made his way over to the spade table. "What's up, homie?" Bo greeted him.

"Shit. Chilling. Somebody got next?"

"You got it. You gamble?"

"Yeah, but I ain't got no store yet. I got plenty bread on my kiosk though. If you know somebody that will 2 for 1 me, send them my way."

"In fact, *I* do. How much you need?"

"What y'all playing per game?"

"Really, it's up to you. We can do $2 a team, since you ain't went to store yet."

"In that case, Imma grab $6 2 for 1. That way, I can play a couple games."

"That's a bet," Bo told him as he left to grab the money. After Bo and Brown Sugar successfully cleared the table, everyone called it a night. Bo finally had a chance to talk with the young dude. "What's your name again?"

"Lil Scrap."

"Where you from?"

"I'm from the East. Pine Trails." Bo figured that. Lil Scrap was Meme's little brother's homeboy. Bo used to see him, when he would slide through late night to scoop Meme up.

"Oh yeah. I'm from the West," Bo lied. "I slide through the East every now and then. I got a few lil thots out there."

"Straight up? Who you be fucking with?"

"You know Meme?" Lil Scrap got excited.

"Ovastood, I know Meme. That's my nigga's older sister. I ain't gone lie. She's bad," Scrap confessed. "Who else you be fucking with?"

"Well, I don't really fuck with her, but what her home-girl Ty been up too?"

"Aww man. She outta there. Thotted out the game. I was at a party a few months back. I'm looking for the restroom and fucked around and walk in on her getting tag-teamed."

Bo's heart fell to his dick. He tried to hide his surprise, but knew he was unsuccessful. "Tag-teamed? You sure?"

"Of course. You know she fuck with Meme tough. I used to be over there when she used to spend the night. I done seen her naked damn near a hundred times. She used to always high side on a young nigga. Whole time, the bitch taking dick in both pant legs," Scrap reported.

Bo couldn't believe it. His heart ached something serious. The lump in his throat wouldn't move. Once Lil Scrap saw Bo clam up, he decided to hit the shower and get ready to rack up. Bo tried to call home, but still didn't have any money on the phone. He wished he could have added money to his account, straight from his books.

It'd been almost two months since Ty paid the phone bill. He could have understood if she didn't have money, but damn. She was out there bussing it open for niggas, and she can't at least be able to keep the phone on? If not for her, at least for him to talk to his kids.

Speaking of kids, she hadn't brought them to see him in almost four months. Now, he saw the real. He'd been fucking with Ty since they were kids. Never would he have thought she was out there like that. He understood that she may have stepped out from time to time, but nothing like this.

Bo laid in his bunk reminiscing about Ty. "Hey, Bo. What's wrong? You look like you wanna kill a motherfucka." Brown Sugar interrupted his thoughts. Bo snapped out of his trance.

"Oh. It ain't nothing. My bitch ass baby momma on some foul shit." Bo shook his head in disappointment.

"Man. That's fucked up. But to be honest, you're better off without her. You're a real nigga and you need a real motherfucka on your team that can benefit you." Bo just nodded in agreement.

"Yeah, but I've been fucking with her since we were

kids. It's just . . . I don't know. I guess at the end of the day, I'm locked up. She gone do what she gone do. Fuck it!"

Bo took his shirt and uniform pants off. He laid under his blanket in nothing but his boxers. With his eyes closed, he reminisced about the free world until he drifted off to sleep.

Ty's pussy felt warm and tight as she squatted over Bo, her hands on his chest, twerking on his dick. Her walls massaged his shaft. Her ass cheeks tapped his balls with every down stroke. She tightened her grip and began to milk him for all he was worth. "Give me that nut, baby. Let me feel that cum all in my pussy." *Damn. Her pussy felt so hot, so tight, so real...*

Bo opened his eyes. Brown Sugar knelt beside the bunk, with his small hands wrapped around Bo's dick, stroking him sensually. "What the fuck you doing?" Bo screeched.

"Ssshhh. Just let me do this for you. Everybody's asleep. It won't take that long. Plus, I'll shoot you $500 to your account tomorrow. You need this, Bo. You're too stressed out. I just wanna make you cum, and that's it. I can feel your nut about to pop. Just a couple more minutes Bo . . . And you'll have $500. Please, let me do this." Brown Sugar begged while he continued to stroke Bo's cock.

Bo looked around. Everyone was asleep. Their bunks were positioned in the blind spot. The picket couldn't see them. Bo was utterly confused. He knew for fact that he wasn't gay. He never once had thoughts of being with a man. But he couldn't deny the fact, the shit Brown Sugar was doing to him felt good as hell.

His balls ached. His rod was as hard as titanium. He closed his eyes and pictured Ty's fat ass pussy gripping his dick. He might have been tripping, but he swore he felt something hot and wet cover his dick head. Squeezing, while sucking him deep. He was too scared to open his eyes. Afraid of what he might see.

He balled his fist up and imagined Ty going to work. Deep-throating his dick with precision. Bo began to tremble and groan. His nuts cracked and shot through his shaft. He jerked a few times.

Bo waited until he felt his dick had been abandoned. He peeled his eyes open. Brown Sugar sat on his own bunk, licking the remnants of Bo's cum off his hands. Bo looked down and saw his flaccid dick twitch, before tucking back into his boxers.

Without so much as another word, Bo turned around and put his back towards Brown Sugar. Before he knew it, he was sleeping like a baby. Finally stress-free for once.

———

It had been three days since Chief was taken into custody. Due to the seriousness of the crime, he was treated like an adult. His birthday was in a week, so the authorities elected to leave him in the adult tank. Marcus hadn't had an opportunity to retrieve the drugs and guns yet, but knew he needed to move fast.

Due to Keon's statement, it looked like Chief was going to be gone for a long time. Laura was always gone, either working, or out looking for a good lawyer. She hadn't really had any time to chill.

As Marcus sat on the porch listening to Lil Baby, Laura pulled up into her driveway. She hopped out, looking sexy as hell in her work attire. Even from thirty feet away, Marcus could see her juicy bubble butt swaying in her business skirt.

She popped the trunk and began grabbing out grocery bags. Marcus got up, and headed to go help her. "Hey, Ms. Laura. You need some help?"

Laura looked at him with a slight smile. "Sure, honey. Thank you so much."

"No problem. Matter of fact, go ahead and relax. I'll get the rest of them groceries. I know you've been going hard for Chief lately. You probably ain't have no time to let your hair down or kick your feet up."

"Boy, you ain't never lied. Oh, well. I'll go ahead and jump in the shower, while you finish up out here." She turned and walked into the house. Marcus's dick began to stir. He still remembered the day she ate him up, while her son laid asleep a mere few feet away.

Ms. Laura was a boss freak. Marcus wanted desperately to see what the pussy was like. After he brought the groceries in, he began to put them up. Just as he was finishing up, Cindy came walking in.

Cindy was a smaller replica of her mother. Smooth caramel skin, B cups and a nice jiggly booty. Cindy drove all the niggas at her school wild. "Oh. What you doing over here?" Cindy was startled to see Marcus at the house, since Chief wasn't there.

"I was helping your mom get the groceries," Marcus explained.

"Where is she?"

"I think she said she was 'bout to hop in the shower. She just came home when I saw her grabbing the bags out of the trunk." Cindy looked at Marcus for a second as if trying to decide something. Before she could speak up, Laura appeared, wrapped in a towel.

"Oh. Cindy. You're home early." Laura was surprised to see her daughter.

"Yeah. They canceled dance practice and I don't have to go to work until five p.m. I'm 'bout to take a nap. Then, I'll be out of your way." The way she said it, gave Marcus the impression that he was on the outside of an inside joke. Cindy looked at her mom up and down.

"Oh, my bad y'all. I just climbed out of the shower. I heard some voices and I . . . . Anyway, let me put on some clothes. Marcus, don't leave yet. I need to talk to you about that situation with Calvin."

"Oh, okay, Ms. Laura." Marcus walked into the living room and waited. He was interested to see what she had to say. Cindy peeped their interaction and gave him a weird and knowing look, before retiring to her bedroom. Marcus sat and wondered. What was all *that* about?

Five minutes later, Laura entered the living room dressed in a pair of brown tights and a light blue baby tee. It was evident she didn't have on a bra. Her nipples protruded like two Hershey kisses. She sat directly in front of Marcus, forcing him to try and *not* stare at the gap between her thighs.

The tights were jacked all the way in her crack. Her meaty sex lips were very prominent. Laura allowed him to get more than an eyeful before she began. "So. I found a lawyer for Calvin. He said based on the statement and eventual testimony of that boy, Calvin could get ten years. I just don't understand. If he's supposed to be this so-called respectable gangsta, how could he give statements on my son? Calvin told me he didn't do it, but Cindy told me you were here, when she told Calvin about that boy putting his hands on her."

Marcus was hoping she didn't ask the question. "So . . . I have to ask. Do you know anything about this?" Marcus hated to lie to Ms. Laura. She was always so welcoming to him. But if Chief told her he didn't do it, then Marcus couldn't, and wouldn't break the code.

"Naw, Ms. Laura. I don't, but I did hear about ole boy beating up on Cindy. In my opinion, he got what he deserved." Laura took a deep breath and exhaled.

She caught Marcus's eyes, drifting back and forth between her thighs. She inched them open, just a little bit further. Marcus emitted a soft groan. His dick began to swell. "You know, Marcus. You and I have unfinished business." Marcus's eyes met hers. "My daughter's here, but I want you to come by later tonight. I'll be able to take care of that hard-on you got right now."

Marcus subconsciously grabbed his piece. Wanting badly to open up his jeans, and relieve the pressure. Laura stood up and walked over towards him. His heart thundered. His hands trembled. It was something about her that always had him off kilter. Laura was a full-grown woman. She made him nervous as hell, but he was up for that challenge.

She stood between his legs and whispered, "Come here." She grabbed his head, placing it next to her crotch. "You smell that, baby? That's a clean grown woman's pussy right there. You smell how wet you're making me right now? I want you to come back tonight, and show me how good that young dick is."

Marcus stuck his nose in her crease and inhaled deeply, gripping on her fleshy cheeks in the process. Laura moaned as she held his head firmly, yearning, burning to have his tongue French-kissing her clit.

"Momma . . . Momma," Cindy yelled.

The two broke away, just as Cindy entered the living room. "Do you know where my AirPods are?"

Without turning, from fear of Cindy seeing the wet spot at the crotch of her tights, Laura responded. "It's in the kitchen drawer. You left them on the counter last night."

"Oh, okay." Cindy took off once again.

Laura bit her bottom lip and eyed Marcus hungrily. "Come back tonight so we can finish this." He nodded, waiting for his dick to deflate on its own, so he could make an exit.

Once he got home, he wasted no time, going straight to his room and jacking his dick until he unloaded one of the fattest nuts in his young life. He started to feel unsure if he could satisfy such a high-powered freak. So dominant, but sexy at the same time. He knew his dick was big enough, but he didn't know if his stroke was deep enough.

One thing he was sure about, he needed to grab the shit from out the attic. And later that night might be his only chance.

*Later that night*:

"Oooh, baby. This young dick is sooo fucking good." '*Smack*!' Marcus smacked Laura on her right cheek, watching it jiggle as he pounded her from the back

They'd been at it for the last hour and a half. Her freak was no match for his stamina. Since they began, Laura came five times and was working on her sixth. Marcus felt her velvet walls gripping his tool as he pulled out and slammed back in. "Ooh shit. Ooh shit. Damn it, boy. You gone make me cum again," Laura wailed.

Marcus gripped her long hair, wrapping it around his fist. He pushed her head into the king size mattress. '*Clap. Clap. Clap. Clap.*' Her booty cheeks crashed against his abs. He leaned in, giving her the business.

Laura tried unsuccessfully to handle it. She had never had someone fuck her with so much power. So much intensity. Eventually, she caved in. She went from being on her knees, to laying flat on her stomach, as Marcus continued his onslaught. Her body began to shiver, as if it was twenty below zero. "Oh my Jesus . . . Lawrd, I'm finna cum again . . . Fuck!"

Laura's coochie spasmed, squirting back onto Marcus's balls, leaving them slick and soaked. He continued to stroke steadily, looking down between them, his dick coated with her vanilla shake.

Marcus pulled back, gripped his dick and slid it up and down the crack of her ass, leaving it wet. "Oohh, baby. I don't think I can take anymore of this dick," Laura pleaded. Her pussy throbbed something serious. The pain felt so delicious.

"Open that ass up," Marcus growled. She obeyed.

Laura reached back and spread herself open for him. He allowed his dick head to sit at her rosebud opening.

With his hand gripping himself at the base, he added a little pressure, pushing the helmet through her barrier. "Oh my Lawrd. Damn, boy. What the fuck?" Marcus pushed his whole dick head in, plus an extra inch. "Oh ssshit. It's been a while, baby. You gotta take it easy on momma. Marcus pulled back and slammed home. "Awww fuck!"

Laura released her ass cheeks and gripped onto the sheets. Marcus pushed the majority of his dick up her back-door, his palms on her lower back, the back of his thighs resting on the backs of hers. She had no choice but to lay there and take everything he was giving her. '*Clap. Clap. Clap.*' Laura's cheeks clapped around his cock. Marcus shoveled in and out of her rectum.

She cried and bit into her pillow. He continued to ride her hard. The sight of her juicy booty wobbling around was too much for him. Before Marcus knew it, his nuts cracked and popped. "Fuck! I'm finna nut, Ms. Laura . . . Shit!" Laura couldn't answer back. She was busy having her own earth-shattering orgasm.

With her face stuffed into the pillow, screaming her release, Marcus withdrew himself. As soon as his dick was able to breathe, it threw up. Globs of white cum splashed all over her brown globes and her lower back. "Agh. Agghh, shit . . . Fuck!" His twitching cock rested between her ass cheeks. Marcus struggled to catch his breath.

His chest heaved as he stared down at Laura. She laid flat on her stomach. Her asshole gaped wide open. Cum covered her soft, brown ass cheeks. And she was completely knocked out! He wouldn't have believed it, if he didn't hear her snoring like a baby bear.

Marcus eased off of her, slipped on his boxers and gym shorts, and made his way up to the attic. He just hoped the drugs and guns would be all in the same spot. He saw old-school basketball cards, picture albums and holiday decorations. Finally, he found the trash bags.

He grabbed everything and carefully exited the attic. He debated on whether or not to check in on Laura. He did. She was still sleeping. He tiptoed past her room and into the backyard. He didn't want anyone to see him leaving out the front, so he threw the bags over the fence and into the backyard of his foster home. Five minutes later, he had the bags hidden in his room.

He hurried back over to Laura's house. Took a quick wash off and crept back into her room. She was still in the same position. Flat on her stomach. Legs cocked open. Just the sight of her had his dick beginning to rise. Her pussy was just as he thought it would be. Plus, she knew exactly how to work it.

Marcus slipped off his shorts and boxers. Stroked his dick until it was fully erect. He positioned himself between her legs. Guided his dick towards the mouth of her pussy and with one powerful shove, he was once again balls deep in her oven-hot snatch. Laura woke up with a moan, as Marcus stroked her to yet another mind-blowing orgasm.

## 5

"MR. BOWMAN. I really think I can beat this case, but the State is offering thirty years for the plea deal." Bo looked at his court-appointed lawyer, an older black man by the name of Carter, and frowned.

"Thirty years! For something I didn't do? Naw, I ain't fucking with that."

"Well. We made the motion for a speedy trial, so if you don't want the plea, I'll tell the judge we're ready to rock and roll."

"So. You really think we can beat this?" Even though he professed his innocence, Bo wasn't so sure.

Carter smiled. "I do. They have a video of a man at the store with the same build as you, but the camera never caught his face. Now. The only thing they have concrete is the fact the man was getting into a late model Malibu that matched the description of the same one you own. But, how many people in the city have that same make and model? They also uncovered a Houston Texans ball cap in the

backseat. The suspect happened to have that same type of
cap on. Once again, how many Houston Texans fans do we
have in the city? On the surface, it looks bad. But once you
dig in, you see everything is circumstantial. At the end of
the day, it's up to you."

Bo took a second to reflect. He was no stranger to the
system. There were countless amounts of men and women
who were actually innocent, but got railroaded by the
system. Just believing he was innocent didn't mean he
would be found innocent. But 30 years was too long. "I
really don't have any choice but to go to trial. They talking
'bout thirty years. I can't sign for that!"

"So, trial it is?"

"Yeah. Tell them I wanna go to trial." With that, Carter
got the reset papers and the Bailiff sent Bo back to his tank.
When he returned, Brown Sugar was waiting on him with a
bowl of food. Fish balls, Cajun style rice, with a soda and a
slice of cake.

Since the first night, Bo had been allowing Brown
Sugar to perform sexual acts on him for money wired to his
books. Even though Bo tried to justify it by saying it was a
business transaction and he wasn't gay, deep down inside,
he knew that he had sold his soul. "Hey, Daddy, how did it
go?"

Bo sat on his bunk exasperatedly. "I'm 'bout to go to
trial. They offered me thirty. I ain't fucking with it."

"Well, does your lawyer feel you will win?"

"That's what he says, but you know how that shit goes."
Brown Sugar nodded. Everyone knows, court-appointed
lawyers will tell you anything to get a check. Before he
began to eat, Bo went to the phone to try and call Ty. *Still*

*restricted.* He hadn't talked to her or the kids in almost a year.

He hung the phone up and stood there thinking. Lil Scrap pulled up on him. "What's good, big homie? What they tell you?"

"They ain't talking 'bout shit. Thirty years," Bo told him.

"So wassup? You gone fight 'em?

"I ain't got no choice. I ain't 'bout to sign for no thirty."

"Ovastood. Well, keep your head up," Scrap said as he turned around to leave, giving Bo some space.

"Appreciate it." They dabbed each other. Bo then made his way back to his bunk. Brown Sugar had his bowl and spoon ready. Bo started eating. *Life can be crazy as shit. I'm locked up for something I ain't do and the only person that's in my corner is a punk I just met,* Bo realized.

He wasn't perfect by any means, but he felt he had done enough good in the world to have at least a little support. "You feel like playing some spades?" Brown Sugar asked, trying to provide some type of distraction.

"Naw. I ain't feeling it right now. Really, a nigga tired. I've been up all morning. 'I'm 'bout to take me a nap," Bo told him while stripping down to his shorts.

"Okay, Daddy. Do you need me to wash any clothes for you?"

Bo thought about it. "My socks and boxers. Oh yeah, my thermals too."

"I got you." Brown Sugar collected the items, while Bo closed his eyes and allowed sleep to take over him.

It seemed like Bo was asleep for fifteen minutes, when he heard some commotion. "You got me all types of fucked up. Yeah, I take dick, but I ain't no pussy, motherfucka!" Bo was half asleep, but he swore it sounded like Brown Sugar yelling at someone. He opened his eyes. Sure enough, it was.

Two weeks prior, there was a new house who everybody called Miami. Miami had been in Houston for only three weeks before they jammed him up on a robbery charge. Since he was from out of town, he really didn't have any support. So, he bullied inmates for their food and hygiene.

Apparently, while Brown Sugar was washing, Miami went over to his bag and took some things out of it. Brown Sugar had caught him in the act. Now, they were face to face, going back and forth. "Say, bitch. You better get out my face with all that, before I crack your jaw." Miami really wasn't trying to fight a punk, but he wouldn't hesitate to knock one out if they got out of line.

"Nigga, give me my shit back. You broke ass niggas always on this type of timing. Get some money, fuck nigga." 'SMACK!' Miami smacked the taste out of Brown Sugar's mouth, causing him to fall and slide next to the pisser.

Before anyone realized it, Bo jumped up out his bunk and with lightning quick speed, cracked Miami's jaw with a thunderous right hook. Miami fell backwards, already asleep. But Bo had already flipped the switch.

As soon as Miami hit the ground, Bo crouched over him, raining down vicious and powerful blows. Blood gushed from each cut Bo's knuckles opened up. When he stared down at Miami, he only saw Ty. All the hate, anger and disappointment was channeled through his fist. He saw the DA's face. The Judge's. He continued to pummel him. Each blow was sent with malice. "Bo! Bo! Stop!" Brown Sugar grabbed Bo's arms and pulled him back. "Don't do it. You'll kill him. He's not worth it."

He snapped out of his rage. Bo looked around the day room. Everyone was staring. He looked towards the picket. Quite a few officers were yelling into their walkie talkies. "Fuck!" Bo screamed. This was the last thing he needed.

Brown Sugar grabbed his face and looked him in his eyes. "Thank you so much, Daddy. I love you for real for real." Brown Sugar kissed Bo on the lips and said, "I got you. That's my word." Everyone gasped at the emotional display. Many already suspected. But seeing it live was still a shock.

Bo was taken back by the kiss. He looked around and caught the disgusted look on Scrap's face. Lil Scrap shook his head and walked back to his bunk.

Seconds later, a group of officers rushed into the pod. They handcuffed Bo and escorted him to the holding cells. In a few hours, he would be reclassified and reassigned to a segregated pod on the 7th floor.

It didn't take long for Lil Scrap to reach out to the world and let them know, Bo was in the county playing in that mud. Of course, the first call he made was to his right-hand man, Mayo. Meme's younger brother.


Meme couldn't believe what she had heard. Mayo's homeboy Scrap called from the county, talking about Bo was in jail messing with homosexuals. Her skin began to crawl when she thought about all the times she sucked his dick, or let him fuck her in the ass. If Bo was gay or bi, she never noticed it.

As she sat in bed, dressed in nothing but a black thong, she played on the phone. Pulling up her social media apps. She didn't hesitate to drop the storyline: *Guess who from the East turned gay in the county?* She sat back and watched as 600 tapped in. In a matter of seconds! When she finally dropped the name, there were countless people who just couldn't believe it was Chad Bo.

They all wanted to know, where's the proof? Meme went on to tell them about Mayo calling from jail. How he swore on his set that he saw it with his own eyes. "What you doing?" T Dub asked, while gripping and massaging his dick slowly.

T Dub was one of Corey's homeboys. Matter of fact, T Dub was one of the two men that were in the bed with Ty when she woke up. That night at the party, Corey was bragging about how good Ty's pussy was. When T Dub saw how drunk and fucked up Ty was, he couldn't resist bussing her shit open.

Him and his cousin fucked her so good, she let them do whatever they wanted to her, leaving her unconscious and drenched in cum. When Corey told him how fire Meme's pussy and head game was, it was only a matter of time before he got a hold of her.

Now, he was at her dingy ass apartment. In her bed and she was playing on her phone. "You remember my girl Ty?" Meme asked him as he jacked off standing over her.

"Yeah. What about her?"

"Her baby daddy in the county fucking with punks." T Dub's dick instantly shriveled up. The first thing that crossed his mind: *If he's gay. And that's his baby momma, they could both be sick.*

"What? So, she fucks with a nigga that fucks around?" Meme saw the look on his face and understood his concerns. She had the same worries.

"I don't think he was fucking around out here. I think it's some shit he just started doing in jail." Meme sounded more confident than she really was.

"How you figure that?"

"Man. I've been knowing Bo since we were kids. If he was double dipping, we would have been on to him. Plus, him and I fucked around a couple times. I just got checked last month and I got a clean bill of health."

"Y'all fucked around?" T Dub couldn't believe Meme was so nonchalant about fucking her best friend's baby daddy. Meme caught his slug and tried to clean it up.

"Yeah. I had felt bad about it, so I told him we had to stop messing around." T Dub smirked. *Yeah, a'ight,* he thought.

"Well, fuck all that. A nigga ain't come all the way over her to watch you gossip on the Gram." He pulled at his dick. It began to rise once again. "I'm trynna see what that throat and pussy like. So put the phone down and pick this dick up."

Meme eyed his muscle as it hardened to around 8 inches. Pre cum glistened from the tip. She instinctively licked her lips, pressed *"Live"* on her phone. She was about to show the world how great a dick sucker she really was.

With her phone recording, Meme grabbed his rod. She smiled for the camera, and with one fluid motion, stuffed him into her mouth. She worked him with one hand, while working the phone with the other. She pulled him out of her mouth with a soft "*pop*". "Here. Hold the phone, while I do me."

T Dub grabbed the phone and aimed it at her. Now that she had two available hands to work with, Meme showed him and the rest of the world why she was considered the best shot of head on the East.

## 6

TY WAS on the way to Mickey D's. Just to be able to use the free WiFi. Her cell phone had been due, but she had to decide between her phone and groceries. To her, that was a no-brainer. So, even though she couldn't call, her kids were able to have food for the next week.

Once she got to the restaurant, she ordered from the dollar menu and jumped on her social media page. It didn't take long to stumble upon Meme's timeline. She couldn't believe what she was reading. It had to be some kind of sick joke. *Bo messing around with punks?* No way! She saw the comments, as well as what Meme posted. She quickly slid in her DM.

SoFlyTy: *Man WTF is all this bout Bo fucking wit punks. Y U spreading dat bullshit.*

AllAboutMeme: *What u mean bullshit. Naw Ty. It's Facts. My lil bro ace, Lil Scrap confirmed it. They was in the tank together.*

SoFlyTy: *What u mean he confirmed it. What he say he sposed to have seen?*

AllAboutMeme: *He say Bo and some skinny punk was always playing each other close. That the punk was cooking for him and shit. Then the punk got into wit some nigga and Bo beat the fool bloody behind him. That's why he in lock up right now.*

SoFlyTy: *Look Meme. I know we ain't been on good terms. But please stop spreading rumors 'bout my baby daddy. U don't know if Scrap is just salting him down because they got into it. U all on the Gram spreading this shit like its facts.*

AllAboutMeme: *U know what. U right. I'm a fallback on this shit. What's up wit u though. U still fucked up 'bout that shit wit Corey?*

SoFlyTy: *U was sposed to be my girl. U know I fuck with Corey and u fucked the nigga n e way. Then u do it while I'm passed out. Dat ain't no cool shit Meme.*

AllAboutMeme: *....*

Ty was waiting on Meme's response. Five minutes went by.

SoFlyTy: *U still there or what?*

AllAboutMeme: *My bad girl. My cousin just pulled up. Let me holla at her real quick. We need to catch up. Imma call you later.*

SoFlyTy: *My phone tripping so just hit me on the Gram or the Book.*

AllAboutMeme: *Aight girl. ttyl*

. . .

Ty exited out of Meme's DM and continued to scroll through her timeline. Something caught her eye. She thought maybe she was tripping, until she clicked on the screen name. *MayDayDreDay.*

She scrolled through the pics and noticed this was the same knucklehead she'd caught with her daughter Mya. From the pics, she could tell the dude was definitely grown and had no business with her daughter. She decided to do some snooping and hit him in his DM. She had an idea.

SoFlyTy: *Wassup*

MayDayDreDay: *Wassup wit it. Where u 4rm*

SoFlyTy: *Where I'm 4rm really don't matter. I'm not on that type of time. I wanna talk 2 u 'bout my daughter.*

MayDayDreDay: *?????*

SoFlyTy: *The one u had sucking your lil ass dick the other day*

MayDayDreDay: *LOL. Now we both know ain't nuttin lil bout my dick. I saw u checkin' him out.*

Ty's mind flashed back to that day. The image of his big, heavy dick stained her brain. She felt her pussy twitch. He was right. She was just capping, talking about his piece was little. Truth be told, he was packing way too much dick for a baby girl.

SoFlyTy: *Whateva nigga. Your ass is too young 4 me.*

Ty needed to bait him in, to make sure he didn't lie. Plus, she needed a record of the conversation.

MayDayDreDay: *How u figure dat. I'm 20.*

*I knew it,* Ty thought to herself.

SoFlyTy: *Just cus u 20 don't mean u know what u doing.*

MayDayDreDay: *All u gotta do is call my bluff.*

SoFlyTy: *Boy, If my daughter can handle that dick. U know her momma would turn your ass out.*

MayDayDreDay: *(laughing emoji) FYI Your daughter couldn't handle it. Just ask her.*

SoFlyTy: *4rm what I saw, she handled it pretty well. Unless I missed something.*

MayDayDreDay: *If u really wanna know. She a'ight on the head but can't take no dick. U talking like u want some smoke or something.*

SoFlyTy: *Naw I don't want no smoke. What I wanna know is, why u fucking wit my daughter and she's only 16.*

MayDayDreDay: *What? Get off da bullshit. U know she's 18.*

SoFlyTy: *Nigga that's my daughter? U don't think I know how old she is. Where u meet her at?*

MayDayDreDay: *We met on here. But she showed me her ID.*

SoFlyTy: *And what did her ID say her name was.*

MayDayDreDay: *April something. Man look. I didn't know. Straight up.*

Ty had to shake her head. April was Mya's cousin. Bo's sister's daughter. No doubt, she used her ID. The same type of shit Ty and Meme used to do when they were her age. Still, she wasn't letting the dude off the hook. When she asked him his age that day, he lied and said he was 18. That let Ty know, he suspected Mya was young the whole time.

SoFlyTy: *Look. What's ur number? I'm 'bout to call u. I'm not feeling no grown man fucking my underage daughter.* He sent his cell number. Ty didn't waste any time in calling.

"Hello?"

"Look. Based on this conversation, I'll decide whether or not to call the police. My daughter's name is Mya, not April. And she's sixteen, not eighteen."

"Man, she showed me an ID. It's not my fault," he argued.

"News flash, lil boy. In the state of Texas, the white folks don't give a damn if she showed you a birth certificate. They gone lock your ass up, and you gone have to register as a sex offender for the rest of your life. Unless . . ."

"Unless what?"

"Look. The way I see it. If you go to jail, you'll have to pay for a bond. Which will cost you a couple bands at the least. Plus, a good lawyer will run you about $20-30,000. When all that is said and done, you'll still be found guilty once the jury sees those messages in my DM. So, what I suggest is this. Shoot me something, and I'll forget all about this. But you have to leave my daughter alone. Even though I know her fast ass is hot in the pants, she ain't ready to be dealing with no grown ass man."

Dre got silent. All she could hear was his breathing. He weighed his options out. "How much?"

"Well, I'm checking out these pics of yours. I see you getting to that bag. So, $5,000 shouldn't be too much for you to handle."

Dre smacked his lips. "Come on, man. 5 bands? And you *know* she lied to a nigga and you still trynna hit a nigga 'cross the head."

"Like I said. You either pay 5 bands or 50 bands. It's your choice."

"Well, how do I know you'll keep it a stack and not try and double back and extort a nigga again."

"When we meet up, I'll let you delete the messages from my DM. So you'll know." Dre took a second to think about it. Ty was wondering if he was smart enough to realize, all she had to do was screenshot the conversation and it was just as good.

"A'ight. How do you want the bread?".

"Cash! You know the Mickey D's on Maxey Road and Woodforest?"

"Yeah," he replied.

"I'm there now. You have twenty minutes before I leave."

"A'ight. I'm on my way."

Ty couldn't believe her luck. Just an hour ago, she didn't have a $100 to her name. Now, if everything goes well, she'll have enough to pay all her bills. Plus, have a little something left over.

She thought about the accusations Meme had made against Bo. She just couldn't believe it. Ain't no way Bo was playing in that mud. Bo barely liked to fuck her in the ass. That's why she enjoyed Corey so much. He treated her like a slut. No hole was off limits. With Bo, she had to get him nice and drunk for him to turn all the way up.

She looked at her watch. Twenty minutes had passed, and no sign of Dre. She decided to give him ten more minutes. Seconds later, a candy red Buick Park Avenue swung into the parking lot. His speakers were vibrating her seat.

Dre hopped out, dressed in a black wife beater, and some loose fitting Gucci cargo shorts with the matching flip flops. His Cuban link glistened against his collar bone. She had to admit, he had lots of sauce. He walked into the dining room and she could see him searching for her. She waved her hand to get his attention.

He didn't look too pleased. But why should he? He knew she had the power to ruin his life in the palm of her hand. Literally. Dre sat down across from her. He took a deep breath, reached in his cargo pocket and pulled out a knot. Begrudgingly, he handed it to her. "That's $5,000. I didn't have time to grab all hundreds, so it's some fifties and twenties. But, it's all there."

Ty didn't want to count it out in the store. She suggested they go to her car. As they sat down, Ty got a whiff of his cologne. Her kitty purred. It had been a while since she'd gotten some good dick. Even though she was disgusted with him for fucking her underage daughter, she couldn't help but to wonder if he knew how to slang all that dick he was packing.

She counted out the money. $5,000 on the dot. She pulled out her phone, praying she parked close enough so the WiFi would work. She had. She allowed Dre to delete the entire thread of the conversation they had in her DM. "A'ight," he said as he reached for the door handle.

"Hold up! I got one more *request*. Dre looked at her inquisitively.

"Wassup?"

"Look. I know you're probably fucked up with me behind this, but I'm actually doing you a favor. You made a horrible mistake that could have ruined your life. I just made it go away for the low. As long as you stop fucking with Mya, I'm good. I know she lied to you. I'm from the streets, so I know how that type of shit goes. But, it doesn't change the fact, it's illegal. You'll be the one under the jail."

Dre simply nodded. He fully understood where she was coming from. Even though he didn't like the fact that she was basically extorting him, he had to respect the real. She let the facts soak in. Then, she continued. "Now that we have an understanding, I'm trynna see if you can back up what you was talking earlier."

He leaned back, surprised. Then he began to smirk. "Oh yeah? So, what you trynna get into?"

"We can dip off to the room real quick. Let me see what that young dick is all about."

"Shit, I'm down. Just let me jump in my whip and I'ma follow you to the room." Dre hopped out with a new pep in his step.

Ty watched him and whispered to herself. "Bitch. You're out of line. You know that nigga's too young to handle all this good ass pussy." She waited until he jumped in his slab, before she pulled out in front of him. Three minutes later, they were at the *Choice Inn*.

Five minutes after that, Ty was on her hands and knees. Dre's dick was punching the back of her throat. "Damn, girl. Eat that dick up," he hissed.

Ty pulled him out of her mouth. "The first one, I want down my throat. But the second one, you choose." She stuffed him back in and began to bob her head. She was going so hard on the dick, her titties shook and her ass wobbled. She cuffed his nuts, massaging them as she took him in even deeper. Dre's toes curled and popped, as Ty ate him alive.

"Fuck! Imma finna nut. Damn, girl. Shit!" His dick

jerked. The first spurt hit the roof of her mouth before skating across the top of her tongue, then sliding down her throat. His cum tasted sweet. That made Ty's pussy get even wetter.

She moaned as he emptied the rest of his load. Ty allowed the last drops to pool on her tongue. She opened wide, displaying the evidence, before she swallowed and it was lost forever.

Dre was amazed. He just got the best head of his young life, and Ty knew. She continued to suckle on his crown lightly, while she spoke to him. "That's what you. *Lick.* Call that grown. *Suck.* Woman head. *Lick.*"

Once he was back hard, she reached into her purse, grabbed a Magnum and rolled it onto him. With his dick standing straight up, Ty straddled his stomach. He could feel her immense heat singe his abs. Her pussy juice felt like warm piss, driving him crazy.

Ty bit her bottom lip, peeked back, grabbed his dick and sat back onto it. "Sssshit," he hissed as her pussy swallowed him with ease. Her ass cheeks sat on his nut sack. She began to rock back and forth slowly.

"Damn, boy. I feel that thing all in my stomach." Ty put her palms on his chest, leaned forward and began to pop that ass on his dick. '*Clap. Clap. Clap. Clap.*' Her ass cheeks crashed against the tops of his thighs. Ty rode him like a racehorse.

Dre reached up with his right hand, grabbed her throat and squeezed tightly. Ty's pussy locked around his shaft. She came with a howling shriek. Her juices rained down, drenching his balls. Dre slapped her on the ass. "Let me hit that from the back." Ty leaned forward. Dre's dick fell out of her snatch, still dripping wet.

She assumed the position. Dre got behind her, peeling her cheeks apart, rubbing and smacking them in the process. Ty looked back at him. "Don't play with the pussy, lil boy. If you gone put it in, make sure you do momma right."

Dre grabbed his dick, sliding it up and down her crease, making sure he tapped her little button every time. Ty moaned. Her pussy got wetter and wetter. "Aww fuck," she moaned as he slammed down into her snatch. With his hands gripping her hips, Dre pulled her towards him, fucking her with all his might.

Ty's titties swung wildly. Her walls caved in as Dre continued to pummel her insides. "Ssshit. That's it, baby. Fuck that pussy for momma. Beat the shit up," she urged as her nut came crashing down on her. "Oh my Gawd. Oh my Gawd. I'm cumming again."

"Yeeaahh. Talk that lil boy shit now," Dre taunted as he worked her pussy like a seasoned porn star. Ty pounded the mattress as she came back to back. Dre looked down. Her pinkish brown asshole was winking at him. The sight was too much.

"Shit! Here it cums! Fuck! Here it cummmsss," he growled.

"Put it anywhere you want, baby." Dre pulled out and snatched the condom off. Jacked his dick a few times, aimed at her ass crack and skeeted right between her globes.

"Awwwwwww fuuuuccckkk," he howled as his heavy balls emptied. He was thoroughly drained and feeling light-headed. Ty wiggled her ass as his cum dripped onto the bedspread.

She looked back at him. "I know you done. When I was twenty years old, sex was a three-hour event. At least."

Dre grabbed his dick, stroked it slowly. "Come get it back up, then put it down."

"My pleasure, lil daddy. You ain't said nothing but a word." Ty grabbed a hold of his dick and sucked her juices off. Dre was back hard as a pipe in no time. They spent the next two and a half hours fucking each other's brains out.

## 7

TY FILLED out the visitation slip, gave it to the deputy, then made her way to the elevators. She pushed the button to the 7th floor and rode the crowded elevator all the way up. Since she was at the jail, she kept it comfortable. But still sexy.

She was clad in BCBG jeans that fit like a glove, showing off her moose knuckle. A pink Prada shirt, with glitter across the front. She took notice of a younger woman and couldn't help but feel like she was the baddest bitch in attendance, despite her age.

Ty approached the central picket and gave the deputy her visitation slip. "Ma'am. You'll have to wait for him in the attorney booth. He's not in GP." Ty had almost forgotten that Bo was supposed to be segg'ed up for beating some nigga half to death behind a punk.

She didn't believe it at first. Now, it seemed like there was some truth to it. They ushered her to the booth. She waited nervously. She honestly didn't know what she was going to say to Bo. They had been messing around, more than half their lives. Never did she suspect or detect any homosexual activity. Suddenly she heard keys. The door opened up. In walked her baby daddy.

Bo was shackled up. Hands to feet. Still, he had the aura of a powerful man. Ty couldn't really read his face, but it looked as if he wasn't too pleased to see her. "Hey, baby," Ty meekly greeted him.

He gave a slight chuckle. "Baby? Oh yeah? I didn't notice. Where the fuck have you been, Ty? Why you up here to see a nigga now?"

"Bo, I know you probably fucked up with me. You have every right to be. To be honest, it's been hard as hell out here without you. I damn near lost the apartment. My phone had gotten turned off. I'm still looking for a job. Mya's out here driving me nuts."

"Why you ain't bring my kids up here to see me?"

"I don't know. I guess I didn't want them to see you like this."

Bo shook his head. "Cut the bullshit, Ty. You got a million excuses. Why are you up here now? What has all of a sudden changed?" Ty took a second to gather her words. She didn't know how to broach the topic. So, she just came right out and said it.

"The streets talking 'bout you in here fucking them boys." His head snapped back as if he'd been slapped.

"Say what?" Then Bo began to laugh. "So that's what brought ya trifling, thot ass up here?" Now, it was Ty's turn to look offended.

"Thot. Thot? Nigga, when the fuck did you start disrespecting a bitch like that?"

"Ever since I learned about you getting flipped at a party a few months back." The look on Ty's face let Bo know what he'd heard was indeed true.

"Who told you that bullshit?"

"It doesn't even matter. You and I both know it's the truth."

"Whateva, nigga. You just pulling shit out your hat, 'cause I pulled up at your doorstep with that gay shit. You don't even have the courtesy to *ask* me if it's true. You heard some shit, and now it's Big Facts?"

"That's what you think? Okay. First and foremost, I love pussy. Always have and always will. Second. If I had a punk in here, it's because my baby momma abandoned me, while I'm fighting this fraud ass murder wrap. Do you know I didn't have any hygiene? A nigga couldn't even wash his ass properly. I don't ask for much. But the little bit I do ask for, you act like you can't fuck with a nigga. Then, I gotta hear about you getting flipped. What happened to the money you were supposed to put on my books? Huh?"

Ty thought back to the day she gave Corey that $100 she was supposed to put on Bo's books. He said he would give it back, but never did. She couldn't do anything but hold her head down. Bo was absolutely right. She had abandoned him.

She could have dropped something on his books. She could have definitely brought the kids to come see him. She made a promise to him, right then and there. "You're right, Bo. I'm all the way out of line. I give you my word that Imma do better. Starting today. Imma put some money on your books, and Imma bring the kids up here to see you next weekend," she assured him.

"Look, Ty, I don't wanna hear about it. I wanna see it. Until then, I'm doing me! Surviving in this bitch. I'm finna go to trial in a few days."

Before she could ask "what that meant", the guard came to get him. "Bo, I'm coming up here this weekend with the kids," she assured him. Bo simply nodded, then left.

Ty's heart was heavy. Bo was truly the love of her life. She took him for granted. She should be there for him in his darkest times. She made her way through the lobby. She was so caught up in her thoughts, she almost forgot to put the money on his books. She rushed back in and tried to deposit $500. The machine said the limit was $300, so she put $300 first, then $200.

When she got in the car, she saw she had a missed call from Dre as well as one from Meme. She called Meme first. They decided to go out to eat, so they could reconnect and work out their problems. Ty told Meme how she just left the county visiting Bo. "I asked Bo about the accusations."

"What did he say?" Meme was anxious to know. Unbeknownst to Ty, Meme had been fucking Bo for a very long time. She even had an early pregnant scare, but Bo paid for the abortion.

"That the shit ain't true. He was fucked up with me for asking."

"I thought about it," Meme admitted. "You were right. Ain't no telling what he and Scrap had going. Scrap might be on some low key hating shit and wanted to salt Bo down."

"That's exactly what this is. But anyway, what time do

you wanna hit the Garden?" Ty was ready to reconcile with her bestie.

"How 'bout seven-thirty? I got a few errands I gotta run, but we can rock out then."

"Seven-thirty it is then."

"A'ight. Talk to you later."

Ty hung up and called Dre. As soon as he answered, she didn't hesitate. "What you doing? . . . Okay. Well, I need some dick real quick. Just tell her you need to go to the store. I'll meet you at the Shell and you can hop in my car. So yours won't smell like sex when you get back . . . I'm on the way." Ty needed a steady supply of dick on call. Dre was the perfect candidate.

His dick was long, fat and he had a very decent stroke game for a dude so young. Ty'd been schooling him. So now, Dre was making her cum in buckets. She checked her purse to make sure she had enough condoms. Then, she made her way to the shell.

———

Marcus was now on his own. He'd been living at a motel for the last couple weeks. Laura offered to let him stay with her so he could "help" around the house. He would have, but he had the weed and guns and didn't want her or the cops to end up finding it. The only logical solution was to get a room. Until he had enough to get an apartment. He paid for a month. Up front.

Marcus sat on the bed in a pair of red and black basketball shorts, no shirt. Scrolling through his phone. Trey had hit him up, talking about he needed more P's.

After negotiating, Marcus agreed to sell him the rest of the stash at $500 a pound. They decided to meet in Trinity Gardens. An apartment complex named Parker Square.

He checked his G-Shock. 2:30. The meet up was scheduled for 3. Marcus didn't have a car of his own, so he asked Laura to help him rent one. He got dressed, grabbed the duffle bag full of weed and jumped in the rental.

As he made the exit off Parker, he felt a sudden chill but dismissed it. Even though Trey was really Chief's homeboy, Marcus still considered them to be cool. He didn't feel like he'd be on any fuck shit. Still, Marcus couldn't shake the eerie feeling in his gut.

He pulled into the complex. Two young niggas dressed in royal blue, with blue bandannas hanging out their back pockets, were posted up out front. Marcus didn't know if he was tripping, but it seemed as if they hopped straight on the phone as soon as they saw him pull in.

He watched them in his rearview, while pulling up to apartment 2812. He parked. Marcus texted Trey to let him know he was outside. Trey told him to "come on in". Marcus grabbed the big duffle and approached the front door.

As soon as he walked in, he felt something was off. The apartment looked like it was vacant. No furniture whatsoever. Trey was standing against the wall with a scowl on his face. "Wassup, Trey?" Trey didn't respond. Instead, he gave a subtle nod. Before Marcus could turn and see who Trey was nodding to, he felt a crushing blow to the side of his head. Then, his world went black.

"Aggghh, fuucckk," Marcus groaned as he awoke, a sharp pain attacking the side of his head. He felt the carpet against his face and smelled the stale air as he began to stir. His head felt as if it weighed a hundred pounds. His heart could be heard beating through his temple.

Marcus tried to remember exactly what happened. As he sat up and looked around, it all started to come back to him. Trey set him up! He looked down and realized his pockets had been turned inside out. He forced himself to sit up.

It took a few minutes for him to regain his balance. But once he did, he made his way out of the apartment. He prayed the car was still there, but wasn't surprised when he saw that it wasn't. Now, he was stuck on the Northside. In someone else's hood. No phone and no way home.

His head was throbbing. Dried up blood was caked down the side of his face. His scalp had a gaping gash. He did the only thing he could do. Walk.

As he approached the front of the complex, he noticed a light-skinned female who looked to be about thirty-something. Marcus couldn't help but to appreciate her beauty. Even in a pair of green jogging pants and an Old Navy shirt, she was bad as hell

Marcus had a thing for older women. He wanted to approach but also knew he wasn't in the best shape to do so. He elected to miss that tackle. Instead, he walked out of the complex and took the long journey home.

Fifteen minutes later, as he walked down the feeder road, Marcus felt a car creeping up his blind side. He didn't want to look back, just in case it was Trey or one of his homeboys. "Hey. Do you need a ride?" A woman's voice yelled over the wind and traffic. Marcus turned and saw it was the same woman from the apartments.

"Uhh. Sure, but I don't have any money," Marcus told her honestly.

"That's okay. I figured you needed help."

Marcus shrugged, then jumped in the passenger seat. "Thanks."

"Where to?"

"Can you take me to Normandy Inn Motel? It's on I-10 and Normandy."

"Sure. I happen to know where that's at . . . I'm Diane, by the way." She extended her hand.

"Oh. Yeah, my name is Marcus. Nice to meet you."

"Nice to meet you as well. How old are you, if you don't mind me asking?"

"I just turned seventeen a few weeks ago."

"Seventeen?" Diane scoffed to herself. "I would have never guessed you were so young. You're built like a grown man."

Marcus looked dejected. "But I *am* a grown man.

"Oh really?" Diane smirked at his statement. It was something about him that had her drawn. But, he was just *too* young. "What happened to you?"

He flipped the visor down, so he could assess the damage. "Some dudes jumped me. They took all my stuff. Even the car I was renting."

Diane shook her head in disappointment. "Do you know who they were?"

"Yeah. One of them. But, it's all good. Even though he was young, Marcus knew enough about the streets. The less you say, the better. They stopped at a light. Diane took a second to study young Marcus.

"You want something to eat real quick, before I drop you off?"

"You don't have to do all that."

"Naw, it's no problem, honey. It would be my pleasure," Diane assured him.

"Well. In that case, sure . . . Thank you."

"What you want to eat?" she asked him.

Marcus didn't know why he said it. But his response was, "What I wanna eat, they don't serve in the restaurant."

Diane wasn't sure if that was a slug or not, so she elected not to respond. Marcus sensed her uncertainty. "How 'bout some fish and fries," he suggested.

She smiled. "Fish and fries it is." The two of them chose to dine at a *Mom and Pop* fish joint. While they ate, they got to know each other. Marcus discovered Diane had no kids, no man, and worked at the Post Office. She seemed cool as hell. They agreed to keep in contact with each other.

Since Marcus got his phone stolen, Diane bought him a "To Go" phone from Wal-Mart. She wanted him to have a way to contact her and vice versa. Diane didn't drop him off until well after midnight. Even though his day started shitty as hell, Marcus had to admit that he may have struck gold with Diane. Only time would tell. One thing he was sure about, though, was that he had to do something about Trey. In the streets, you never allow a nigga to do what Trey did to him. He just didn't know how he was going to handle it just yet. Marcus took a hot shower, laid in bed and fantasized about his guardian angel, Diane.

. . .

The trial had been going on for a few days now. Bo had longed since picked his jury. Now, the state had put on their witnesses. The store owner, an older, dark-skinned, pot-bellied Nigerian named Abel Nkamahi, was addressing the court.

Everyone in the hood just called him Mr. A., and Mr. A had been the manager at the store two months prior to the murder. His dad was the owner and previous manager who ran the store since Ty and Bo were kids. He had served them their first pack of cigarettes when they were just 15 years old.

Mr. A looked unsure about getting on the stand. Once he was sworn in, his testimony began.

DA: Mr. Nkamahi. *Can you please state your name for the record?*

Mr. A: *Abel Nkamahi.*

DA: *Mr. Nkamahi, where are you employed?*

Mr. A: *I work at the Circle A gas station on Woodforest and the Beltway.*

DA: *Were you working on the night of March 29, 2024. At approximately 9:00 p.m.?*

Mr. A: *Yes. I was.*

Ty heard the date and realized that was Corey's birthday. That night, she and Corey shacked up at his apartment. Fucking each other's brains out.

DA: *Do you remember that man (**pointed towards Bo**) ever going into your store?*

Mr. A: *I remember his vehicle pulling up and parking in front of the store. He got out with his football cap on.*

DA: *Do you remember what he purchased?*

Mr. A: *Yes, ma'am. He purchased some grape flavored cigars, some skittles and a bag of chips.*

Ty's heart beat began to gallop. Her skin felt like bugs were crawling all over her. *Bo hates flavored cigars.* She was always the one buying them. When she did, it was *always* grape. *Her favorite!* Images of Corey coming back from the store that night, with grape Phillies, skittles and a bag of chips, flooded her memories.

She knew Bo couldn't have had the car that night. Because she stayed at Corey's up until 3:00 am. She even had Meme cover for her. Telling Bo, they'd been at the club all night. Something in the back of her mind was gnawing at her. She refused to believe it, but there was no other explanation.

DA: *Mr. Nkamahi, I'm about to show you the surveillance video for that night.*

The State's attorney turned on the monitor. Immediately, Ty knew the truth. She watched as the Malibu pulled up to the store. You couldn't see the entire license plate, but the first three digits were visible.

Ty, as well as the jurors, watched as a man matching Bo's description exited the vehicle and entered the store.

Due to the Houston Texans ball cap, the suspect's face wasn't visible. But Ty knew exactly who it was. She knew him down to the size of his dick. She watched in horror as Corey left the store. Something caught his attention.

They watched as the suspect dropped his items and took off running. As if he was chasing someone. Moments later, he returned, jumped in the car and fled the scene.

Ty began to hyperventilate. Bo was innocent. She was the only one in the courtroom, besides Bo, that knew that to be fact.

Her leg wouldn't stop moving. How could she fix this? How could she tell Bo that the nigga she'd been cheating on him with was the one that committed the murder he was on trial for. Her palms became clammy. *Corey killed that man and came back to bed like it was nothing,* she thought as she stared at her baby daddy. Her stomach tied in knots. She became light headed. Ty couldn't breathe. She needed air.

She stood up and walked out the courtroom. As she was making her way to the restroom, she felt her strength leaving her. Ty stopped and placed her hand on the wall for support. Her breath was shortened. Her knees were weak. She attempted to take another few steps, but her legs gave way. Ty collapsed face first. Right there in the hallway.

# 8

Bo sat in his single-man cell, thumbing through his pictures. He still couldn't get over the fact that he'd lost the trial. He'd always heard of innocent people getting slammed by the system, but to actually be one of the statistics was devastating.

On top of that, Ty had passed out at the courthouse. He hadn't heard from her since. He didn't know what caused her illness, or if she would be alright. Now that he had been sentenced to life, he needed her support more than ever. 'Tap Tap' "Bowman. You gone eat?" The 6'5", redneck officer stared at Bo, waiting for his response.

"What is it?"

The officer looked down at the tray. "It looks like fear factor." Bo shook his head.

"Naw, I'm good." He really didn't have an appetite. He felt lost and abandoned. By his family and friends. By the system. He laid back in his bunk, allowing the tears to fall down his face.

Before he knew it, he'd fallen asleep. Two hours later, he awoke to find an envelope on the floor. He picked it up. It was a letter. It took a second to recognize the name on the return address. *Brown Sugar!* Bo sat and stared at the envelope for minutes, before he decided to open it. He was trying to figure out, what the hell would Brown Sugar want to write to him about?

A part of him really didn't want to know. Another part of him felt he owed Brown Sugar at least that much. Brown Sugar was the reason he had what he had. He was also the reason he was able to go to the pen with money on his books. He opened up the letter and read:

*Dear Bo,*

*Surprise! I know you're probably like OMG, but I told you I would hold you down. I put some money on your books. I saw that you went to trial. I wish I could have been there. I just got released last night. They dismissed the case. Don't worry about it, babe, I'll make sure you have a good appeal lawyer. I've already started looking for one. If you put me on your visitation list, I'll come see you. No matter where they have you housed. I'll hit that highway for you. I know all this is new to you. If you're willing, then I will walk you through it.*

*You were there for my darkest time. I'll be there for yours. Before I leave, I want you to know that I fell in love with you. I know you don't feel the same way, but I'm not tripping about that. I'll be there for you regardless. Hold your head, take care of yourself so I can take care of you.*

*Sincerely,*

*Sugar!*


Bo read the letter three more times. *What the fuck is going on?* He didn't know what to do, or how to react. He was far from gay. Or was he? If he was completely honest with himself, he cared for Brown Sugar. Sugar had done so much for him. And, it sounded like he wanted to do even more. Could Bo really have a relationship with another man? A year ago, that would have been a *hell to the fuck naw,* but now . . . Bo made the decision. He grabbed the pen and began to write back


*Hey Brown Sugar,*

*I really appreciate your letter. No matter what anybody says, you've kept it one hundred with me the whole time we've known each other. To be honest, all this is new to me. I never would have ever imagined myself dealing with another man. I can't even believe I just wrote that. Anyway, real is real. And you're one of the realest I've ever met. I will put you on my visitation list and I hope you set up the phone so I can call. Thank you for the money on my books. Because of you, I'll have everything I need. I can't promise you that I will fall in love with you, but I will say that I won't allow outside influences to dictate us. So, with that said. Thank you once again and I look forward to us building.*

*Chad Bo*

Bo stuck the letter in the crease of the door for mail pick up. He surprisingly felt better. Just the fact he had someone solid in his corner made the time a lot easier. He closed his eyes and thought about his kids. How would they feel about him dealing with homosexuals? He couldn't believe it. Out of everyone in the world . . .

———

'*Beep . . . Beep . . . Beep.*' Ty began to stir, awoken by the constant beeping coming from the machine. She opened her eyes. It took a minute for her vision to return. The first person she saw was Meme playing on her phone. No doubt, she was scrolling through her social media apps. "Meme," Ty croaked, throat parched, dry as the desert sand. Meme still hadn't heard her. Too engaged on what was trending. "Meme!" She said it louder.

Meme picked her head up. She saw Ty finally awake and smiled. "Heyyy, girl. You had a bitch scared to death."

"What happened? The last thing I remember is being at Bo's trial. Wait. I need to get out of here. I have to go back before his trial is over with," Ty said frantically.

Meme grabbed ahold of her hand and squeezed. "Ty. Bo's trial is over with. They found him guilty. He got life."

"What! What you mean he got life? How did they find him guilty? He didn't do it! He's innocent, Meme. Damn, this shit is so fucked up." Ty was hurt and confused. Now that she knew who the real murderer was, she felt sick to her stomach. She was partly responsible for her baby daddy being falsely accused.

Meme felt Ty was in denial when it came to Bo. She just kept her mouth shut and offered the emotional support she needed. Plus, she had some more bad news. Ty read Meme's expression and knew something else was on her mind. "How long have I been up here? Bo's trial had just started when I passed out."

Meme took a deep breath. "Baby. You've been in a coma for two months."

"What?"

"Yeah, girl. They had you on the machine for about a month. They decided to take you off, but you kept breathing on your own by then."

"Wait. Where are the kids? My apartment?"

"Ssshh. Calm down, girl. You lost the apartment, but your kids are safe. They're staying at my apartment right now. Your car's parked and all your shit is in storage. Ty breathed in a big sigh of relief. She was grateful to have Meme as a friend. Men come and go, but true friends last forever.

"Thank you so much, Meme. I don't know what I would do without you."

"Don't worry 'bout that. You're my bitch. You know I'll always have your back." Meme patted her on the back of her hand, just as the doctor came in.

Doctor Jordan. A middle-aged black man with salt-and-pepper hair, chestnut colored eyes and a warm smile, approached her bedside. "How are you doing, Ms. Jackson? I see you're finally back with us."

Ty smiled at him. "To be honest, Doc, my whole body hurts. I was hoping you could tell me if I'm alright or not." Doctor Jordan glanced in Meme's direction.

"Well, girl, let me get to the house. Let me know if you need something," Meme said as she got ready to leave.

"A'ight. Um, can you tell the kids I love them and I'll see them soon."

"Of course. I'll bring them with me next time."

"No! I don't want them to see me like this," Ty protested. Meme nodded in understanding.

"A'ight girl. Talk to you later."

As soon as Meme made it out the door, Ty stared at Doctor Jordan. "Just give it to me straight, Doc. I'm a big girl, I can take it."

"Very well, Ms. Jackson. We did some blood work. It turns out, you have SLE. *Systemic Lupus Erythematosus.* It's hereditary, so there's no cure. But, it can be treated."

"Hold up! Say what. Lupus, what's that?"

"Well. Lupus is an immune disease that basically tricks the body into believing your organs are the enemy host. So, your immune system begins to attack your organs until they fail."

"So. Basically, I'm 'bout to die."

"Well. Technically, we all die, Ms. Jackson, but you can live a long time with Lupus. With the right medication and diet, but that's not the worst of your problems," Doctor Jordan informed her.

Ty's head snapped back. "You mean to tell me it gets worse than that?"

"Well, the thing is this. Due to the Lupus, your immune system doesn't have enough white blood cells to fight off multiple diseases at once. And um . . . We've detected a form of cancer."

Ty's eyes shot open in shock. "Wait, wait. What? You're saying I have cancer?" Ty began to tremble. Her chest felt tight. She could barely breathe.

"We've detected Stage 4 Pancreatic cancer. Sometimes, a person can go months or even years without having any symptoms. Unfortunately, the Lupus sped the process up. So, that's why you fainted and went into a coma." Ty couldn't believe her ears. She didn't understand why God was being so cruel to her. She'd lost everything. Now, she was going to die. Tears began to pour down her cheeks. She struggled to hold them in, for fear that when the dam broke, she would lose herself. She took deep breaths to try and steady herself. "So, what's next, Doc?"

"Well. With treatment, chemotherapy among other things, you may be able to fight it off for a couple more years," Doctor Jordan advised her.

"What if I don't want to take the treatments?"

"You'll have 6-8 months. Tops." Ty wasn't feeling the idea of going through chemo. She watched her paw paw go through hell fighting prostate cancer. She made a promise to herself, she wouldn't allow her kids to watch her go through that.

But without treatment, the doctor said she'd only have 6-8 months to live. Her heart hurt like hell. The only thing she kept asking herself: *what are my kids going to do?* Neither one of them was old enough to get a job.

Her tears began to flow more freely. The doctor saw she was struggling to maintain her composure. He decided to give her the privacy she needed. As soon as he closed the door behind him, she broke down in sobs. She cried her eyes out. Not for herself, but for her children. And for Bo. Because of her, they were all suffering. Whether deliberate or not.

At the end of the day, she was responsible for their troubles. She made up her mind, right there in that hospital bed. If she only had eight months to live, she'd live to the fullest. She'd do right by her family and when it was time to go, she'd know they would be alright.

———

Marcus peeked through the blinds and watched as Trey jumped into a candy blue 96' Buick Roadmaster. Unbeknownst to Trey, Marcus had been watching him for a week now. Shortly after getting the ride from Diane, he called her up and they went out to eat. Afterwards, Diane brought him back to her apartment, where he fucked her into submission.

He sexed her so good, she offered him a place to stay. Even though she claimed it was free of charge, Marcus was smart enough to know he had to pay her with good dick when she needed it. Which apparently, was twice a day.

Diane likes to suck dick and get fucked right before work, and late at night, right before bed. Of course, Marcus didn't mind. Plus, staying at her spot gave him a perfect place to gather Intel.

He never left the house, so he didn't have to worry about anyone knowing his whereabouts. Through his investigation skills, he learned Trey stayed with his baby momma. A thick chocolate chick, with small breasts and a fat ass. They had a little boy together.

Every day at 2:30 p.m., Trey would pick up his son from school. The baby momma would leave to go to work two hours later. Apparently, she worked at a nursing home. She wouldn't return home until 2 in the morning.

Each time his baby momma would leave for work, Marcus watched as Trey walked over to his neighbor's apartment, which happened to be his baby momma's best friend. A redbone, slim chick with reddish brown hair and a nice little bubble butt.

Trey would greet her at the door, grab her ass and tongue her down, before she would let him in the apartment. His 9-year-old son would be left at home alone, while he was next door fucking his neighbor's brains out.

Then, Trey would return a few hours later to put his son to bed. Once his son was tucked in, Trey would return to the neighbor's until around midnight. After a while, he would be seen sauntering back to his place, where he would remain until his baby momma returned home.

Marcus watched the same routine occur, three days in a row. He was confident, nothing would change. He honestly didn't know what he would do, when he would be face to face with Trey. What he did know, he had to do *something*.

Since that day he was ambushed and robbed, he hadn't been able to get a wink of sleep. Not unless he completely exhausted himself having sex with Diane. The violation ate at him. It infected and festered in his soul. All he could think about was revenge.

He sat in Diane's bedroom window, peeking through the blinds. It was 2:40 p.m. Sure enough, Trey was pulling back up to the apartment. Marcus watched Trey and his son hop out the car and head inside, eager to relax. Marcus checked his watch. He had roughly two hours left before the baby momma left for work. As soon as she departed, Marcus grabbed a knife he'd stolen a couple weeks prior.

He threw on his black hoodie, black pants and black Air Force Ones. He purposely never wore the outfit around Diane. Just in case a description of him would ever be released. He needed her to be as clueless as possible. She was due home at one in the morning.

Marcus had a very tight window to operate in. His nerves began to act up. His guts began to bubble. He couldn't stop passing gas. He went into the bathroom and took a nice long shit. Now that the time was approaching, he wasn't too sure he could go through with it.

He washed up and began to pace. The clock read 9:30 p.m. He checked out the scene. Trey left the neighbor's spot and was on the way to put his son to bed. Soon after, he crept back over to his mistress. *Showtime!*

Marcus left Diane's apartment, walked down the street as if he was walking toward the store. Abruptly, he made a turn and headed back towards Trey's apartment. From observation, he noticed Trey never locked the door. Obviously, to make it easier to go back and forth so frequently.

He twisted the doorknob. Then pushed it open. The door creaked as he stepped in. The apartment was modestly furnished. Leather couches, with a 58-inch flat screen, decorated the wall. Marcus took notice of a family picture propped on the end table. Trey, his baby momma, and their son.

Marcus made his way to the back of the apartment. He prayed like hell that the little boy stayed asleep. There were three different rooms. He checked the first. The bathroom. He checked the second. It appeared to be where Trey and his baby momma slept. The bed was empty. He carefully opened door number three. In the bed, swaddled up, was a tiny figure. He listened to the light snores. The child was still asleep. He hoped for his sake and Trey's, he stayed that way.

He closed the door and contemplated. He knew Trey would be home in an hour or so. He needed to get ready. Marcus went into Trey's bedroom and hid under the bed. He figured Trey would need to come home and take a shower after going a couple rounds with his side bitch. Afterwards, he would come in and lay down. Too tired to give baby momma any dick when she got home. That's when Marcus would strike.

Sure enough, Trey returned and went straight into his room. After dropping his drawers, he grabbed a towel and went straight into the master bathroom. Marcus crawled from underneath the bed, heart pounding, nerves jumping.

He placed his back flat against the wall, waiting for Trey to emerge from the bathroom. The shower stopped running. He pulled the knife out and gripped it repeatedly. He steadied his breathing.

Seconds later, Trey emerged with nothing on but a towel wrapped around his waist. As soon as Trey walked past Marcus's line of sight, Marcus grabbed him by the neck. Administering a vicious chokehold.

Trey began to struggle and fight. He was surprisingly strong as an ox. Not to mention, in fear for his life. Trey slammed Marcus against the dresser, knocking everything down to the floor. Marcus tightened his grip, but Trey continued to sling him around.

In fear of waking up the son with the noise, Marcus brought the knife down with a vicious swing. A wet thud could be heard as the blade opened up his intestines. Marcus picked it up and delivered another blow. This time to his sternum. Then his chest. Repeatedly, until Trey shivered. His heart struggled to pump enough blood to his limbs. The missing blood decorated the majority of the bedroom. Trey wheezed, his lungs devoid of oxygen. His body went limp as Marcus continued to squeeze with all his might.

Even after Trey's body ceased movement, Marcus refused to let go. Twenty seconds after death, Marcus continued to squeeze. Trey's body hung in his arms, dead weight straining his muscles. He allowed Trey's body to fall. It did, like a wet noodle to the ground.

Marcus's chest heaved. He checked his clothes. Blood splatters decorated his attire like paint balls. He needed to hurry up and get out of there. He heard a soft voice outside the bedroom door. "Daddy?" Marcus froze. He didn't want to kill a kid. But the child was old enough to point at trial.

He tried his luck. He put his hand over his mouth. "Go back to bed, son. Daddy's about to take a bath." Marcus crossed his fingers, and hoped the little boy bought it. He put his ear to the door. Another door could be heard being shut. Relief consumed him.

Marcus slowly opened the bedroom door, then he rushed out. Leaving the apartment in haste, he hurried down the street to the corner store but didn't go in.

Instead, he ducked behind the building and found the spot where he stashed another set of clothes. He changed into them, grabbed the lighter fluid, doused the hoodie, jeans and Air Forces. He lit the match and watched everything burn to a crisp. Then, he buried the knife in a separate location.

After he was satisfied the evidence was destroyed, he hurried back to Diane's apartment. As soon as he made it in, his whole body relaxed and he nearly fell over from the relief. Marcus hopped in the shower and scrubbed himself clean.

Fifteen minutes after he showered, Diane came home to find him "asleep" in her bed. She woke him up with some head and wouldn't stop until he fed her loads of his cum.

After licking her lips clean, she looked down at him as she undressed. "I'm about to take a shower. I need that dick up and ready when I return. You understand?"

"Of course," Marcus obediently replied. "I got you, baby." Diane went to take her shower and Marcus couldn't resist the urge to go to the window and take a peek at Trey's apartment. His baby momma should be returning soon. When she finds his body, all hell will break loose. Marcus laid back in bed watching porn on his phone, waiting for Diane to come get her late night fix.

'*Knock! Knock! Knock!*' It was 4:30 a.m. Someone was beating on Diane's door. Both her and Marcus were sound asleep, after another magnificent round of freaky sex. Marcus was the first to hear the knocking, but wasn't about to answer it. For one, this wasn't his apartment. For two, he felt he knew who was at the door and he didn't want any parts of that.

He slid his hand in between her thighs and cuffed her thick, meaty sex lips. She stirred as she heard the knocking. "What the . . . Who? What time is it?"

Marcus feigned as if he was disorientated. Diane begrudgingly got up out of bed. After throwing on a terry cloth robe, she stalked towards her front door. "Who is it?"

"It's the police, ma'am. We need to speak to you."

"Police?" Diane couldn't think of any possible reason the police would be at her crib. She swung the door open and was greeted with a female plain-clothes Detective.

"Good morning, ma'am. I don't mean to bother you, but did you happen to see anything suspicious across the street late last night?" Diane looked behind the detective. Multiple cop cars were parked up and down the driveway.

The neighbors across the street had their door wide open. Officers were going in and out of their apartment. "Uhh. No, Detective. I've been at work all night. I came home around 1:30 a.m. and I've been asleep since."

"Are you home alone?"

"I live by myself." The detective let her choice of words dance around her head for a little bit

"Okay, ma'am, well . . ."

"What exactly happened?"

"One of your neighbors was murdered late last night."

"Oh my God," Diane covered her mouth in shock. "Was it the man, or the woman?"

"The male," the detective answered.

Diane hugged herself. She knew Trey very well. When she first moved to the apartments, Trey used to come over while his baby momma—Ashley—was at work. Diane would ride his dick into the ground. She even let him bring one of his homeboys over and they had a threesome for his birthday.

Then, Diane's schedule changed. She started working the same hours as Ashley, and Trey stopped coming over. "How did he die?"

"I'm sorry, ma'am. I can't tell you that. This is an ongoing investigation. Did you know the victim?"

"Sort of. I used to see him around. Him and his girlfriend."

"So, you never spoke to him?"

"Of course. The occasional, *how you doing*? Etc." Detective Gordon wrote something down in her notes.

"Okay. Well, if you can think of anything else, please contact us." She brandished a card and handed it to Diane. "Where did you say you work again?"

"Oh. I work at the hospital. Hermann Memorial. I'm an RN." Gordon wrote that down before she excused herself. Diane closed the door and headed back to her bedroom.

"What was all that about?" Marcus laid in bed, stroking his dick slowly. Diane licked her lips and disrobed. She crawled back into bed and reached for his piece.

"One of my neighbors got killed last night," she said as she stroked him methodically.

"Killed? Damn. Who was it?"

"This dude that stayed across the street named Trey."

Marcus could sense a certain sadness about the way she said Trey's name. "Were you cool with him?" He had to ask.

"We used to mess around. Nothing serious though."

That was definitely news to Marcus. He didn't allow it to fluster him. Instead, he reached for the back of her head, pulled her face into his lap and fed her an early morning snack. While Diane topped him off, he decided it was time to move around for good. As soon as she went to work the next day, he called an Uber and went back to the motel.

## 9

TY WAS WALKING AROUND, eating and using the restroom on her own. Still, the hospital refused to discharge her. She decided to say fuck it and made an escape.

Three days ago, she asked Meme to bring her a set of clothes, and park her car in the hospital parking lot. She didn't know when she would make her move, but she knew she needed to be ready. The day came, when the opportunity presented itself.

She waited until shift change. She knew from experience that the staff that came at 10 would be lazy and wouldn't be paying attention. She got dressed, grabbed her car keys and casually walked out of the room.

Five minutes later, she was in the parking lot. Now, she had to find her car. After hitting the alarm several times, she finally heard what she was looking for.

Ty jumped inside her Malibu and cranked up the engine. As soon as she did, memories of Bo taking her to go buy it at the car lot flooded her head. She gripped the wheel, guilt consuming her like a blanket. She needed to go see him. She didn't want to compound on his stress, but she also knew that he needed to know. She had less than a year to live. His kids would be out there without either one of their parents. She put the car in drive and headed to her best friend Meme's house.

Ty pulled up to Thorntree Apartments and felt nostalgic. Ever since she was a kid, Thorntree had been like a second home. She had countless fights, met many people, and for as long as she could remember, Thorntree had been the home of her best friend.

She pulled into the parking lot and parked next to Meme's Nissan. Ty sat back and laughed as she remembered the time her and Meme were two deep, chasing down some nigga Meme used to mess with, all over the East.

Supposedly, she found a text message in his phone where he was telling someone that Meme ate his ass out and he was going to try and run a train on her the next time they messed around. To say she wasn't pleased would be an understatement. Ty chuckled as she remembered Meme chunking a brick through the dude's windshield when they finally caught up to him.

She hopped out and made the walk over to Meme's apartment. She smiled when she saw her son—CJ—outside playing with some nappy head little boys from the complex. He hadn't seen her yet. She just stared at him for a minute. He looked so happy. It made her smile.

In life, you have to cherish the smiles. Sometimes, you feel as if they are as rare as Blood Diamonds. CJ must have sensed something, because suddenly he looked up and caught sight of her. Instantly, he stopped what he was doing and ran into her arms. "Momma! You're home."

She scooped him up and gave him a great big hug. "Heyyy, baby . . . I've missed you."

"I've missed you too, momma. Are you gonna stay with us?"

"Yeah. Momma's gonna stay with you. Then, we'll get our own place. You want to go see your daddy this weekend?"

Little CJ's eyes lit up. It felt like Christmas. He hadn't seen his dad in a very long time. "Pleeaasee momma. Let's go see daddy!"

She put him back on the ground. "Okay. We'll go see him this weekend. Where's your sister?"

CJ put his head down and solemnly said, "She's inside with her friends."

Ty picked up on something strange. "What friends?"

"I don't know momma. Some man."

Ty's face instantly contorted. "Man! Wait here, CJ. I'll be right back." She stormed towards the apartment. She was about to knock. Something told her to try the door knob. She twisted and pushed it open. What she saw, she couldn't believe.

Her daughter sat next to a man that looked to be in his forties. His pants around his ankles, dick out, she jacked him off feverishly. The apartment smelled like weed and sex. "Bitch! What the fuck do you think you're doing?"

Both Mya and the man jumped, startled by the intrusion. "Momma?"

"Momma hell. Bitch, if you don't get your fast ass up. Where's Meme?"

"Uh . . . Uh. She's in the room." Dude began pulling up his pants.

"Say, look out, lady. I don't know you, but you can't come up in my home girl shit like this. Man, you tripping," the old-school told Ty.

Ty snapped. She ran into the kitchen and grabbed a butcher knife. "Nigga, I'm 'bout to cut your dick off, you pedophile motherfucker. Your ass is probably older than me "

He threw his hands up. "Hold up. Hold up. Don't do something you gone regret."

Mya jumped between her mom and her old-school sugar daddy. "Momma. Please don't hurt him."

"Girl. If you don't move your nasty ass out the way, you gone fuck around and make me cut your ass up too," Ty seethed. The man saw a chance to escape. He bolted out of the apartment. Pants and belt still unbuckled. Ty was enraged.

She turned and headed to Meme's bedroom, kicking in the door. Meme was face down, ass up. Some middle aged black man was hitting her from the back. As soon as they heard the door buss open, they saw Ty barging in with a butcher knife.

Dude jumped out of the pussy. Dick slanging. Still wet with Meme's juices. "What the fuck is this?" he yelled as he backed up into a corner.

Meme crawled up the bed. Her back was against the headboard. "Ty. What the fuck is going on?"

"Bitch. You got some grown ass man in here messing with my daughter?"

"Huh? What are you talking 'bout?" Meme seemed as if she was confused. "Look. Just put the knife down so we can talk and get to the bottom of this."

"Talk? Bitch, I trusted you with my kids. This the type of shit you got going on? I don't wanna do no talking." Ty wanted to hurt somebody.

"Look, Ty, everything can be explained. Just put the knife down. Please!" Ty was gripping the knife so hard, her knuckles turned white. She didn't give two fucks anymore. She had visions of stabbing Meme multiple times. Until she was drenched in her blood.

"Momma, please. Don't do this. Daddy's already gone. We can't lose you too." Mya's voice broke through. Ty snapped out of her rage.

Her breathing became stable. She dropped the knife. She stared Meme down. Hurt, disappointment and anger swam across her face. "I thought you were my friend. Don't come anywhere near me or my kids," Ty growled. Ty turned around and headed out the door. "Mya, grab you and your brother's shit. We're leaving."

Mya struggled to keep up. "But momma, where are we going?"

"Let me worry 'bout that. You just do what I told you to do. Get y'all's shit."

Ten minutes later, Ty and her kids were loaded up in her Malibu. She didn't have anywhere to go, so she took them to Greenwood Park. "Jr., go play. I need to talk to your sister real quick."

Once CJ was gone, Ty allowed her tears to fall. "Why,

Mya? Why are you so intent on doing this to me? To your-self. You're a baby. Why are you so in a rush to be grown?" Ty stared at Mya. She was a spitting image of her mother.

Mya was ashamed. Not for what she did. Ashamed, 'cause she felt she had gone too far. "Momma. I do what I do to help feed us." That comment smacked Ty right in the face.

"What? What do you mean?"

"You don't think I know we're barely making it. That we barely have enough food to eat. Momma, we are now *literally* homeless. I can't sit back and let my lil brother go hungry. So yeah. If dudes wanna pay me, momma, Imma take their money." Mya reached in her pocket and pulled out $200. She threw the money in the cup holder. "That man at aunt Meme's house paid me $200, momma. I was going to use it to help aunt Meme with the bills, but maybe we can use it to get a room for a week or something."

Ty began to sob even harder. Mya continued with her profession. "I don't do that because I want to, but because I *have* to."

"No, you don't, Mya," Ty tried to counter.

"Yes, I do! If not, then no one else will," Mya screamed. "Daddy's gone and you don't have a job. We wear the same clothes to school almost every day because we can't afford to wash them on the regular. We never have any food." The tears began to pour down the young girl's face.

Ty's heart broke. The fact that her underage daughter felt she had to sell herself in order to feed her family was too much to bear. It was Ty's job to take care of her, not the other way around. She honestly didn't know what to say.

Her daughter was right. How could she sit back and let her brother go hungry. Ty sat and watched as Mya cried her young eyes out. "Sshhh. It's okay, baby. You're right. I'm so sorry. I haven't been doing *my* job. I promise. You don't ever have to do that again. Momma gone take care of everything." That seemed to make Mya cry even harder.

She grabbed her and allowed Mya to cry over her shoulder. Ty made her decision. From that day forth, she would do whatever it took to take care of her family. *Fuck everyone else!*

If she had to rob, cheat, steal or even kill . . . So be it. That night, she took the $200 from her daughter and got a room for a week at the cheapest motel she could find. She also bought groceries for three days and with the little bit of change left, she put gas in the tank.

God had been exceptionally cruel to her ass of late. With her diagnosis of sudden death, Ty had only one mission in life. To make sure before she passed through the world, her kids would have everything they needed. By any means necessary. Clock's Ticking!

———

Ty, while on her knees in a dingy motel room, continued to bob on his dick with precision. She slyly checked the time on her watch. *9:30.* She had another appointment scheduled for 10 p.m. Jason, her 9:30, was only paying her $150 for some top, but her 10 o'clock was coming off $300 for the whole thing.

Dressed in nothing but her black laced bra and panties, Ty went into overdrive. She placed her left palm on his abs, while her right hand gripped the base of his shaft. She tightened her lips around the head of his cock, sucking deeply as she stroked him rapidly. She felt him spasm. His dick hardened even more.

His balls jumped and danced in his scrotum. Ty knew she had him. "Oh shit. Oh shit. I'm 'bout to cum. Bitch. Awww fuck!" Jason bellowed as Ty milked his cock dry. The first spurt hit the roof of her mouth. She quickly pulled him out of her mouth and watched as the hot nut shot forth from the tip, cascading down the side of his shaft, pouring all over her hand.

Normally, she wouldn't allow a good nut to go to waste, but if a trick wanted his cum ate, he had to pay extra. She had two kids to feed and a baby daddy to get out of prison. Jason laid back on the bed, panting heavily. This was the second time he had used her services. Once again, he was thoroughly satisfied.

Ty wiped her hand on the bedspread, stood up and began to get dressed. She glanced at her watch again. *9:40.* She needed to hurry up. She grabbed her purse, pulled out her hand sanitizer and her mouth wash. Once she felt cleansed, she got ready to go. "When can I fuck with you again?" Jason asked, still sprawled over the bed. His dick laid limp against his right thigh.

"Shit. Whenever you have some more money," Ty said over her shoulder as she walked out the door.

For the last couple weeks, Ty had been turning tricks like an Olympic gymnast. She knew it was a dangerous game. Since she didn't have anyone protecting her, she had to be extremely cautious.

As she jumped in her car, she called her 10 o'clock

appointment. A middle-aged security guard by the name of Phil. She'd met him one night as she was leaving one of her trick's apartment complex. After a short conversation, they exchanged numbers.

Ty texted Phil to let him know she might be running a few minutes late. She needed to swing by her room to check on the kids and drop her money off. As a rule, she never brought money on a date. After she let Phil know what was up, she headed "home".

As she turned into the parking lot, she spotted someone coming out of his room. He was tall, strongly built, but seemed young as hell. He was dressed in basketball shorts, a wife beater and some flip flops. Ty made a mental note to check him out later. She needed someone she could depend on when things got rough in the field. You had plenty of creeps out there. Being a woman could only get you so far. Ty watched him head to the front desk. Then, back to his room. She wondered if he was staying, or was he just an overnighter.

She walked into her room and smiled. Jr. was fast asleep. Mya sat watching movies on her phone. Luckily, the cheap motel had at least WiFi. So, even though Ty hadn't been able to pay to keep her line operational at the moment, Mya was still able to enjoy the content.

Since it was summer break, Ty had a few months to find them somewhere stable to live. Ever since their talk, Mya had been on her best behavior. "Here My..." Ty handed her daughter the $150 to put up for her. Mya reached under the mattress she was laying on and pulled out a nylon pouch filled with money.

When Ty started grinding, Mya was responsible for

stashing and accounting. "Where we at right now, baby?" Ty asked while getting ready to go back out the door.

"This will put us at $2,650," Mya answered proudly.

"Well. I'm 'bout to go grab $300 right now, so that will put us right under three grand. I don't have to pay for the room until next week, so we're good on that. I'm looking to get us a house in 5th Ward. They're asking for $80,000 total for it. So . . ." Ty wanted to be able to leave something behind for the kids.

She had six to eight months to do it. Even though turning tricks was paying the bills, she was pressed for time and needed something a little more lucrative, at a faster pace. She just didn't know what.

Ty hadn't told Mya about her death sentence yet. She didn't want her worrying about it. "That's a bet, momma. You're doing your thing. We'll get there." Mya smiled at her. Ty smiled back.

"Well. Let me get back to it. Y'all ate already?"

"Yea, we had ordered some wings. We have yours in the microwave," Mya informed her.

"Oh, okay. Well, I'll eat mines when I get back." Ty turned to leave, but stopped when she thought of something. "My—It's a dude that stays three doors down from us. Have you been seeing him around?"

Mya squinted, as she tried to think. "Oh, yeah. I think I know who you're talking 'bout. He's been here ever since we got here."

"Really?" Ty couldn't believe she hadn't seen him until now.

"Yeah, momma. You know you be gone. So that's why you never noticed him."

"Hmmm," Ty said as she began to walk out the door.

"Be careful, momma . . . Love you." Ty turned and smiled at her only daughter.

"I will. And I love you, too."


Twenty-three minutes later, Ty pulled up to Phil's two-bedroom duplex in South Lawn. Dopefiends and D Boys loitered around out front. As soon as they saw Ty's Malibu pull up, the hustlers assumed she was there to score. "What you need, school?" *School?* Ty felt genuinely offended. Not because they thought she was there to buy crack, but because he basically called her old.

She appraised the young hustler. She guessed him to be in his mid-teens. Brown skin, curly hair with a medium build. She assumed he played sports. "I'm here to see Phil," she told him.

The young hustler smiled. He looked back at the crowd and yelled, "She's here for Uncle Phil." Seeing as she wasn't there to buy any dope, the D Boys lost interest. The young hustler eyed her up and down. "I know my Unc ain't got no girl. Plus, he's known to trick, so you must be working?"

Normally, Ty was very discreet about her business, but having a death sentence made her not give two fucks. "Yeah, I'm working."

The young hustler smiled. "I'm Benny. How much you charging?"

Ty chuckled. "You serious? How old are you?"

"I'm nineteen. Why?

"You got some ID on you?" Ty didn't believe for one

minute the baby face hustler was 19. He looked closer to Mya's age.

"I'm on the run right now, so I don't carry no ID. But on Gang, I'm nineteen. Matter fact . . ." He turned to the crowd. "Say, look out, Polo." A tall lanky, bright-skinned dude turned his head. "Come here real quick." The bright-skinned dude began to walk towards the car. Ty looked at Benny, confused. "I'm not gonna say nothing. Ask him how old I am."

Polo approached the car. Ty guessed him to be in his mid-twenties. She looked up at him from her driver seat. "How old is Benny?"

Without hesitation, Polo responded. "Nineteen"

"You good," Benny told him and Polo sauntered back to doing what he was doing. Ty smirked.

"A'ight. Well, my price depends on what you're trying to do," Ty told him.

Benny licked his lips. "No cap. A nigga trynna do it all."

"Well, in that case, Imma charge you $300. Can you handle that?"

"Momma. I can handle that and *you* without breaking a sweat." Ty smirked at his confidence.

"Well. We'll see. Here, put my number in your phone." Benny did just that. Finally, Phil appeared and escorted Ty through the crowd and into his apartment.

Once inside, he fixed her a shot of cognac. "I hope them youngsters out there didn't give you too much trouble."

"Naw. They good. I'm a hood bitch. It takes more than that to scare me," Ty told him honestly.

Phil smiled. "Well. Here's your money." He handed her

three crisp one hundred dollar bills. She tucked them in her bra and began to strip. For a middle-aged man, Phil had a bunch of stamina. Phil had a thing for giving head and eating ass. He spent twenty minutes doing just that. Ty climaxed three times before he finally strapped the condom on and gave her as much as she could handle. An hour after she had arrived, Phil was laid back, mouth wide, sleeping like a newborn and snoring like a Pappa Bear.

Ty eased out of the bed, and began to dress. As she freshened herself up, something caught her eye. She walked over to the dresser. A gold watch sat underneath a face towel. She instinctively looked back at Phil to make sure he was still asleep. She slowly removed the towel and scooped the watch up gently. *Rolex!* She put it to her ear. *No ticking.*

Ty quickly stuffed the watch into her pocket and hurried out of the apartment. Her heart was sputtering in her chest. She maneuvered through the crowd of hustlers, eager to make it back to her car. As soon as she grabbed the door handle, "Hey. You!" Ty froze. Her hands shook as she turned around.

Benny walked up to her smiling. "You forgot to tell me your name."

"Ty. My name is Ty," she said meekly.

"Well. Check this out. I just came up on $125. You think a nigga can get a lil top for that."

Normally, Ty didn't allow customers to haggle, but she needed to get the hell up out of there. "Um. A'ight. But not here. Do you have a car?"

"Yeah, but I don't drive. I'm on the run, remember? Look, I'll jump in the car with you. We can drive down the street and when we get done, I'll hop out and walk back down here."

"A'ight. Let's go," Ty hurriedly responded. They both got in, and Ty drove off. She parked about two blocks away. Right in front of someone's house.

Before the car was all the way in park, Benny had his dick out, stroking it. "Money first, baby boy," Ty purred.

"Oh yeah." He pulled out a knot and peeled off a hundred-dollar bill, a twenty, then a five. Ty took it, stashed it, then turned sideways in her seat. She took a hold of his dick, stroked it a few times, leaned over the console and consumed him into her mouth. To be so young, Benny had a hefty sized cock.

Ty smelled a light musk as well as the taste of sweat on his balls from being on the grind. It wasn't her first time messing with a hustler, straight off the block.

Benny grabbed the back of her head as she shook him from left to right, inching him deeper and deeper down her throat. "*Acka. Acka,*" Ty choked. Benny clogged up her airway. He held onto her head as he began to work his hips. Fucking her mouth with vigor. '*Ghlup, Ghlup, Ghlup!*'

Ty held on to his thighs, squeezing, as she prayed to taste his cum on her tongue. Benny's body tensed up. He squeezed her head tightly. His nut cracked and shot out his dick head, coating her tonsils. She tried to raise up, but Benny wouldn't allow her to. He held down on her head, forcing her to eat his cum, free of charge. "Awww, yesss. That's it, girl. Eat that dick up." Ty took another gulp and swallowed his last spurts.

Finally, Benny released his grip. Ty released hers. She

smacked her lips, wiping the corners of her mouth. "Nigga. I charge to babysit."

Benny looked at her sheepishly. "Oh yeah? What you be charging?"

"I need fifty more." Ty held out her hand. Awaiting to be compensated.

Benny shook his head. "You lucky that shit was well worth it," he huffed. "A nigga gone have to put you on speed dial." He handed her the money.

Ty put it up, flipped the visor down and checked herself, waiting for him to get out. Seconds later, Benny was out the door and headed back down the street. She put the car in drive and couldn't wait to get back to her side of town.

One thing for sure, she wouldn't be dealing with Benny or Phil again. She reached into her pocket and pulled out the gold Rolex watch. First thing in the morning, she was going to the pawn shop. She didn't give a damn what they would give her for it. Anything was better than nothing.

When Ty made it back to the room, both her children were fast asleep. She hopped in the shower to wash the day away. As she stood under the water, she cried. Not for the things she had to do, but for the fact she had to do them.

# 10

Bo HAD BEEN in the Ferguson unit for three days. His cellmate was a white dude named Brody. Brody was a 6'3", 230 lbs., corn-fed, backwoods redneck, who was also prospecting for the Aryan Brotherhood. As soon as they became cellies, they got the pleasantries out of the way. The likes and dislikes in the cell. The schedules. Basically, how each of them liked to do time. Both had life sentences. In their opinion, they would be seeing each other for quite some time.

On Bo's first day there, dudes were pulling up from everywhere. Some of them had heard his name in the streets and some were trying to find out if he was affiliated with anybody. Bo wasn't a gang member. And at 34, about to be 35, it was too late to join.

He was a firm believer; most gang members are quick to hide behind their set. If you catch them one on one, they'd fold up like lawn chairs.

Bo played the day room the first couple days. Just to make sure niggas knew he wasn't ducking no smoke. On his third day there, a Saturday, he got called for a visit. He really didn't have any fresh whites to wear, so he rocked what he had on.

"Who coming to see you?" Brody asked as Bo threw on his black state boots.

"Shit. I really don't know, most likely my baby momma and my kids."

"A'ight. Well, have a good visit celly," Brody encouraged.

"Appreciate it, man." Bo headed to visitation, looking for Ty. He searched everywhere but didn't see her.

"*Psst. Pssstt.*" Bo turned his head, looking for the source. He saw the last person he really expected to see. *Brown Sugar!*

Bo had been locked up before. He knew in order to get a contact visit, a person had to be an immediate family. So, when he went through orientation, he told classification that Brown Sugar—aka Enrique Ameza—was his brother. "Heyy, Bo," Sugar sang. Bo took one look at him and almost ran out of visitation.

Brown Sugar had his hair long and dyed blond. He had long eyelashes, lip gloss with eye liner around his lips. His clothes were tight as hell. There was no mistaking his sexual preference.

Bo felt extremely self-conscious as he looked around the visitation room. Since he was fresh on the unit, he didn't know who stayed on the block and who didn't. Sitting on the table in front of Brown Sugar, were snacks galore.

Damn near every item from the machine was laid out in front of him. Bo cautiously took a seat.

"What's up, Ricky?" Bo called him by the name he used in the county.

"You surprised to see me?"

"Uhh. To be honest, yeah. A lil bit. You should have told me you were pulling up. I would've tried to get a cut or something."

Brown Sugar made a swatting motion with his hand. "Boy. You know I don't give a damn about all that. Still, I'll let you know I'm coming next time. I really came up here to tell you I set the phone up. I know you ain't got no tablet yet, but when you get one, I'll send you some pics. Also, I talked to the appeal lawyer. He said he wants to wait until your Direct Appeal is over with, then he'll do the 1107. That way, he could add things to the record. Whatever that means."

"What's he gonna charge?"

"Well. He's talking 'bout $40,000, but don't worry 'bout that. I'ma take care of it. I got you." Bo leaned back and analyzed Brown Sugar for a second.

"Why you doing this for me?" Bo had to ask. "You know I got a baby momma. Plus, you already know I'm not gay." Brown Sugar held up his hand.

"Look, Bo, I'm doing this because you're a real nigga. And you deserve it. You looked out for me and never tried to take advantage of that. When you beat that nigga's ass for me, I know you did it because you cared. Not as a lover, but as a friend. I'm that type of bitch, I'll do whatever for my true friends. I'm not asking you to fall in love. As long

as you know how I feel about you, then I'm cool with that.
Right now, I just want to make sure you do your time
comfortably. No stress! I told you I got you and I always
keep my word. Now eat! You look like you done lost
twenty pounds."

Bo laughed and began to chow down. When the visit
was over, they stood up and hugged each other. Brown
Sugar genuinely loved Bo. He had every intention of riding
the time out with Bo. Win, lose or draw. Bo took a whiff of
his perfume, "Nude" by Rihanna. That was the same kind
Ty wore. He shook his head. Brown Sugar was definitely
extra. Bo made it back to the block smiling and riding on
cloud nine.

He didn't even notice the looks he was getting until his
celly asked: "Damn, celly. Why you ain't tell me you
fucked around?"

"Huh? What you talking 'bout?"

"Shit. Old boy Krash came back from visit talking 'bout
you was down there kissing and freaking on some punk."

"Say what? Who the fuck is Krash?" Seeing how irate
Bo had gotten, Brody didn't want to be involved. He threw
his hands up.

"Look. That ain't really my business. I just brought it up
because we live together." Bo shook his head. The anger
began to build. Bo was known for his ill-fated temper. Once
he got going, like a runaway train, he was very hard to
stop.

He hadn't been on the unit a whole week and niggas
were already slandering his name. "Say, let me borrow your
shoes." Bo knew what needed to be done, but he needed
some "rec" shoes to dance in.

"Go ahead." Bo grabbed Brody's New Balances and rushed out the cell as soon as the doors rolled. He pulled right up on this old-school cat named Flex, who knew Bo's old man from back in the day.

"Say, Unc. You know a nigga named Krash?" Flex nodded, already knowing where things were headed. Like everyone else, he'd heard Krash come back and so-called "expose" Bo.

"The nigga over by the sports TV." Bo looked and saw who he was referring to. Krash was a Crip nigga from East Texas who had been locked up for ten years. At 6 foot, 200 lbs., he had a little name for himself. Bo didn't give a fuck about none of that.

He made his way over to where Krash was seated. "Say, nigga. I'm trynna fuck with you." Bo was heated. He understood prison politics and knew he had to give Krash an opportunity to answer the call. If it was up to Bo, he would have just taken off and broke his jaw.

Krash just smirked and looked at Bo like he was beneath him. "I don't fight punks, nigga."

*'WHAP!'*

Bo slapped fire from his ass. Krash toppled over and fell to the floor. The whole day room got silent. Krash was apparently dazed. Bo looked as if he intended to capitalize. "Hold up, Cuz. You ain't 'bout to hit the homie while he's on the ground." One of Krash's Crip homeboys intervened.

"He gone let him up, Nick." Flex appeared out of nowhere. Seemingly, to have Bo's back. In prison, gangs rule. Those that are solo tend to be food. Every now and then, you have a solo that comes through, that's so stiff, so stomp down, that everyone else has to respect him.

Bo backed up a few feet, giving Krash the space and opportunity to get back on his feet. Once he was fully erect and on his feet, he touched his lip and saw he had blood on his fingers. Bo busted his lip. "Oh naw, nigga. I'm 'bout to beat your bitch ass," Krash fumed.

Krash took his shirt off and squared up. He threw two jabs back to back and popped Bo in his mouth. Bo tasted the blood instantly. He honestly wasn't expecting Krash to be that fast. Now, he needed to readjust his strategy.

Bo went on the offensive. He faked a right, Krash flinched, trying to block. Bo dipped up under and caught him with a smooth right hook, splitting Krash's left eye on contact. Krash fell against the wall, but bounced off it with a right straight and a left hook.

He caught Bo with the straight, but Bo was able to slip the hook, ducked and came up with a vicious uppercut that snapped Krash's head back. Before he could recover, Bo dipped his knees and with everything he had and launched a right hook that slept Krash for good.

Krash laid on the floor leaking. Bo stood over him. Chest heaving, mouth busted, body trembling from the adrenaline. "Say, nigga. I'm trynna fuck with you now," Nick huffed. He wasn't feeling how Bo just did his homie. Now he wanted to pick up Krash's slack.

"Say, lil homie. That shit's dead. Krash slandered his name. He had the right to defend that. He did, now that shit's over with." Flex laid the law down. Being 50 years old and a retired Crip, his word held weight on the unit. Begrudgingly, Nick respected the call. He woke Krash up and Bo returned to his cell, furious.

The whole while, a punk named Rose was sitting back

watching it all. He hated Krash with a passion. Krash was the type of nigga that would constantly put dudes on blast for fucking around. That made it hard for Rose to get a boyfriend. He loved to see Krash get his ass whooped. And if the rumors were true, then Bo would be his new man.

## 11

MEANCA "MEME" Thomas was a damaged woman, who was widely misunderstood. She grew up in a single-parent home. She had a younger brother, but he lived with her dad and his new wife. Meme had grown up watching her mom, Samantha, get drunk and parade different men around her daughter. Night after night.

When Meme was only 10, her mom was dealing with a man named Claude. Claude was a working man, didn't do any drugs, and loved Samantha, as well as her daughter. He worked hard to provide and would often spoil little Meme with toys and treats.

Even though Claude was a loving man, it wasn't enough for Samantha. While he was hard at work, she would sneak men over to the house, making sure they were long gone before Claude came back home.

One day, while Samantha was entertaining a local hustler by the name of King Rome, Claude was involved in an accident on the job. Management excused him from work, while they investigated the matter.

Meme was in the living room playing when she heard the keys jingling and the locks being turned. She instinctively looked towards her mom's bedroom, knowing that seconds prior, she'd heard her mom having sex with the man she called Rome. Even though she was young, Meme understood that something tragic was about to transpire.

The door swung open. Claude's face lit up when he saw little Meme in the living room. "Heyy, princess. What you doing?"

"Watching cartoons. Playing with Barbie," Meme replied. She felt an unexplained sorrow overcome her.

"Where's momma?"

"In her room. Can you take me to go get some ice cream?" Even so young, Meme tried to aid and assist her mom in the deception. Trying to convince Claude to leave before things were discovered. Suddenly, Samantha's moans came traveling through the thin walls.

"Oooh, Rome . . . Ssshit. This dick is sooo good. Fuck this pussy, baby." Claude's face dropped. His eyes began to mist. Little Meme reached out and gave him a great big hug. She didn't want Mr. Claude to go. He was the only man she wanted to be her daddy. She could feel him trembling with rage against her tiny frame.

Claude pulled her back and looked into her eyes. A single tear, streaming down his cheek! "Listen princess. When you get older, I want you to be your own woman. Okay? Don't let your momma turn you into her."

"Okay," Meme whispered. She honestly didn't understand what the wisdom he gave her entailed. She just knew it was something important. Claude flinched when he heard the head board smack against the wall. Samantha continued to cry out about how big Rome's dick was, while her 10-year-old daughter played a few feet away.

Claude rose up to his full height, took a couple deep breaths, and made his way over to the bedroom. '*BOOM!*'

With a swift, hard kick, the bedroom door collapsed open. Claude rushed in. Meme was on top of Rome, riding his dick reverse cowgirl. "Oh my God, Claude, it's not what you think," Samantha stupidly claimed.

"You dirty bitch. While your daughter's here?"

"Say, homie. You need to back the fuck up," Rome warned, even though he was in another man's house fucking, another man's woman in another man's bed.

Claude looked at him with disgust. "Nigga, this is my motherfucking house."

Meme heard Samantha scream, "Please stop it. No. No. Don't." '*Bocka Bocka.*' Two shots rang out. Meme jumped up. Frightened, she ran and hid behind the sofa. "Oh my God. Oh my God. Noooo. Please Lord. Don't let him die," Samantha wailed.

"You seen that nigga attack me. You saw that shit. I was defending myself," Rome kept reiterating.

"Please. Just go, Rome. Please!" Meme watched as Rome stormed out of the room, gun still in hand. Even though she didn't fully understand death yet, she felt and knew her world would never be the same again. She would never see Mr. Claude coming through the door with gifts and goodies.

Soon after that, the drinking and drugging got worse.

Samantha would often blame Meme. Saying how she was the one that let Claude in, or that she told Claude there was a man in the room.

Meme watched her mother deteriorate. Until one day, she came home from school and found her mom asleep on the couch. Meme thought nothing of it, until she woke up the next day and Samantha was still in the same spot. She hadn't moved an inch. When Meme was 10 years old, she lost her mother to an overdose.

Soon after, she moved in with her dad's sister—Bridget. Bridget had 5 kids of her own, plus Meme's brand new baby brother by her dad, Mayo. Mayo's mom, as well as their dad, had gotten caught up on a robbery charge and sentenced to 40 years apiece.

With so many mouths to feed, Meme got lost in the shuffle. She spent her middle school and high school years acting out. Sex and drugs were her daily sedatives. She became best friends with Ty, but she never really learned how to love. True loyalty was foreign to her. Every relationship, she sabotaged. Her reasoning: she felt that eventually everyone would hurt her by leaving, like Mr. Claude and her momma did.

Meme was standing by the DJ booth, dancing on her boyfriend Slick. Slick was a D Boy from the West, who met Meme at the mall one day and fell for her. Meme's reputation on the East was stained, so she would opt to "wife" dudes from other sides of town. They didn't know the real her.

The "Tunnel" was the *it* club of the year. They had

plans on partying all night long. Meme was rocking a short, mid-thigh, Givenchy knock-off dress with four-inch stilettos.

Slick leaned back against the wall, as Meme bounced her fat ass, grinding into his lap. He looked down at her booty moving and bit his lip. She rolled him up like a joint. Her dress rode up, exposing the bottom of her ass cheeks. Her booty jiggled to the lyrics of Meagan and Cardi's "WAP".

Out of all the women he'd messed with, Meme had some of the best pussy. But by far, her head game was unmatched. While Slick was focused on her ass, Meme had her eyes on another hustler in the club.

Patrick, or better known as "Pat Pat", was a brick nigga from the Southwest. He was known for making money, but was no stranger to letting his gun go. Well, technically, he hired steppas to let theirs do the talking for him. Pat's name started ringing heavily on the East. Supposedly, he relocated and even had a nephew that was playing ball for North Shore.

Meme knew exactly who he was when she spotted him. He had been eyeing her down, watching her twerk on Slick for the last five minutes. She licked her lips seductively, as she felt Slick's dick rise and harden. Meme worked his shaft and snuggled it between her cheeks, stroking him as she made her ass clap.

Pat nodded, letting her know he took notice. She nodded back. When the song ended, Meme looked back at Slick. "Hey, boo. I'm 'bout to go use the restroom. Can you get me a drink?"

"A'ight, baby, I got you."

Meme took off in one direction, while Slick traveled in another. Meme had to be careful. What she was doing was extremely dangerous. She couldn't help herself. She kept her head on a swivel, as she searched for Pat. Finally, she saw him standing in a corner, with three of his homeboys.

"I'm cool. It ain't gotta come to that. Shoot me your number and I'll hit you up tomorrow so we can finish what we started." Meme rattled off her number, before reluctantly headed back to Slick.

As soon as she saw him, she could tell he was irate. "Meme. Where the fuck you been at?"

"My bad, baby. I had bumped into my girl Treesy in the restroom. I told her ass you was gone be upset. We were in there riding about the Ty and Bo situation. My bad baby. I lost track of time." Meme rubbed him across his chest.

She leaned in and kissed him, while caressing his manhood. Slick moaned into her mouth. "Let's go home, baby. I need some of this dick," she whispered in his ear. Her lips barely grazed his earlobes. Just like that, Meme had averted another bad situation. As she led Slick out of the club, she was thinking about Pat's dick the whole ride home.

Corey had been paying very close attention to Bo's situation. He didn't know if Ty would have figured it out or not, but he wasn't taking any chances. These last few months, he spent basically in hiding. No clubs, limited social media. The only thing he kept constant in his hiatus was pussy. Corey was one of those type of dudes the ladies loved and the niggas hated. Why? Probably because he'd fucked someone's baby momma, girlfriend or maybe even wife.

It wasn't always like that for Corey. When he was around 16 years old, he was madly in love with a beautiful girl who stayed across the street from him. A girl whose smile could light up the sky. A girl who made him tremble when she stared directly into his eyes. Her name was Erica. And she was his homeboy's older sister's friend.

Erica was about 5'5", brown-skinned and 143 lbs. She had a fat ass, a nice set of tits, and a very seductive way about herself. She was also 18. Which meant, she probably didn't even notice Corey.

That didn't mean he didn't notice her. In fact, it seemed like that was all he noticed. Corey's mom had lost her job, so Corey said fuck school and took up hustling, full time. He took to it like a fish to water. The only problem was: he could never stay focused.

One day, he was mowing the grass for his mom, when out of nowhere Erica approached. She was looking so good in her blue jean Daisy Dukes and her cream colored baby tee. Her legs looked silky smooth. Since he started making a little money and gaining a little rep, Corey had sampled a few of the girls at his school, but he still hadn't had anything like Erica.

"Hey, Corey. Where you been at? I noticed you don't be around like you used to." Corey was shocked to hear Erica had been checking for him.

"Yeah. I don't really be at the house. I be on Uvalde damn near every day. If not, I'm in Cloverleaf," he told her.

"What you be doing over there? Ain't nothing but crack and meth in the Leaf."

"Hustling. Shit, a nigga gotta get it in," Corey told her. Something told him she already knew that, but he decided to humor her.

"Look at you. Big time hustler," she said with a smile. The compliment made Corey feel good about himself. He finally felt seen. "Where's your girlfriend at? I know you got one."

Corey did have a little female he was thinking about going with, but he wasn't about to tell Erica that. Instead he said, "Naw. I ain't got no girl. I don't want one. What I need is a woman."

"Oh yeah, is that right? Well, women are high maintenance. Especially a woman worth keeping. Are you the type of man that's stingy with his woman, or will you make sure she's taken care of?"

All his boys balked at the idea of tricking, or spending money on a female. Corey didn't consider Erica just any female. He'd give whatever to make her happy. "I take care of mine. Imma Boss, and if my woman's a Boss, she needs to look like one."

Erica couldn't hold back the smile if she wanted to. That was exactly what she wanted to hear. With a few choice words, Erica got Corey to commit to the idea of them being a couple. A week later, he finally got to experience her velvet folds and her suction cup head. After that, he was completely smitten.

The good thing about it was, finally bagging the girl of his dreams allowed Corey to focus on his hustle. He was able to hold his mom down until she got another job, as

well as moving him and Erica into a condo close to downtown. He copped a five series Benz for him and a 328i
BMW for Erica.

Him and his plug—Pierre—had gotten close. Pierre was
a Haitian cat, who kept that white girl on deck. There was
never a drought, and the ticket was all love. Pierre would
sometimes come to Houston to kick it. When he did, he
would invite Corey and Erica out to party with him. By the
time he was 17, Corey was definitely a six-figure nigga.
Then, all that came to a screeching halt.

It was July 4th weekend. Pierre had come to the city to
celebrate. Of course he invited Corey and Erica to come
party on a yacht with him. Everything was lit. The drinks
were coming in abundance. The atmosphere was live. It
was all love. Corey was having the time of his life. So
much so, he ended up getting so drunk that he passed out.

When he finally awoke, he found himself in a hotel
room. Alone. Not understanding how he got off the yacht,
he called Erica. No answer. He called Pierre. Same thing.
He checked the time and realized it was 2 p.m. He'd been
out for the last 10 hours. His head was pounding.
Something wasn't sitting right, but he just didn't know
what.

He hopped in the shower to shake the cobwebs. When
he dried off, he tried to hit their cell phones again. Same
results. *What the fuck?* He didn't know what else to do but
wait. So he did. 24 hours later, he decided to go home.
When he got there, his heart dropped. Erica had cleaned
him out. Every single dollar he'd earned was gone.

Corey went berserk. He tried calling her phone, but all
he was getting was the voicemail. He had an idea. *Hit her*

*on the Gram.* What he saw crushed his spirit. Live on the Gram, were Erica and Pierre hugged up, kissing. You could tell, they'd been messing around for some time. The familiar way they held each other. The comfort by which they interacted. Right under Corey's nose.

He flashed back to all the nights the three of them spent together. His third eye allowed him to peep the treachery. The innuendos. The side glances. He felt sick to his stomach. He wanted to die. Even more so, he wanted to kill something.

Instead, Corey reverted back to his shell. This time, he made a promise. He would never trust a bitch, or a nigga for that matter. Every female was fair game. If a nigga could fuck his, then he was going to fuck theirs. Since then, Corey's fucked his homeboys' girls, their sisters, their mommas. His philosophy is: *If she's cute and grown, I'll take her home.*

Corey sort of felt bad about Bo getting wrapped up in that murder. For one that Corey committed, over $100. He knew if Ty knew the circumstances surrounding that night, she would put two and two together. She wasn't the sharpest knife in the drawer, but she was far from the dullest. At the end of the day, that's the game. *Better him than me,* Corey thought to himself.

Now that Bo was convicted and sent up the river, it was time for Corey to come out and play. He scrolled through his phone. He pulled up the number of a lil thot by the name of Daja. She was his baby momma's little cousin, and a certified, bonafide freak.

Speaking of baby mommas, Kourtney is the closest woman to a wifey. She's the mother of his two boys, and she's always begging him for a long term commitment. Little did she know, hell will freeze over before that happens. Still, if Corey was completely honest, he did love her. Just not enough to keep his dick out of other people's pussies.

## 12

"Y'ALL LOCK UP. I won't be back until late," Ty told her kids as she walked out of her motel room. She had another date lined up. Two young D Boys from Trinity Gardens wanted to spend a couple hours with her. She usually didn't mess with the young ones. Too much bullshit, but they were talking about paying $500 apiece, so she wasn't about to pass that up.

Dressed the part, in a mini skirt, a mesh top and some heels, Ty was about to jump in the car, when she heard a familiar voice. "Heyyy, Ty!" She turned her head to see if it was indeed true. Sitting in the passenger seat of a royal blue Audi A8, was none other than her former best friend, Meme.

"Wassup, Me? What you doing over here?" Ty was definitely not happy to see her and Meme could tell from her tone.

"Oh. I'm here with my *man.* We just stopped by, to get

us right real quick." Meme leaned back in the seat to give Ty an unobstructed view of Pat.

Black as tar, light brown eyes, spinning 360 degree waves, with full pink, juicy lips, Pat smiled and showed his gold and diamond grill. Ty was stuck. She had to admit, Pat was sexy as hell. While Meme was facing her looking smug, Pat was behind Meme, throwing Ty all sorts of seductive looks. Obviously, he wanted to try what Ty had to offer. She played it cool. "Well. I gotta head out. Nice to meet you, uhm . . ."

"Pat," he answered. Meme turned around and gave him the stink eye. She didn't intend on Ty learning his real name. She just wanted to flaunt him in her face.

"Well. Nice to meet you, Mr. Pat."

"Likewise," he responded. Ty turned around and purposely dropped her keys. As she bent down to pick them up, she knew Pat not only got a good look at her ass cheeks, but also a sneak peak of her plump and juicy pussy. Ty heard Meme smack her lips at the obvious display, but Ty didn't care. Her and Meme were no longer friends, so fuck her. *If you wanted to keep him, you should've never let me see him,* Ty thought, as she jumped in her car.

Ty made it to the trap house on Curry Road around 11:00 p.m. The agreement was, for $500 apiece, she would service both of them until 1:00 a.m. She didn't like turning tricks at houses she wasn't familiar with. Because, nine times out of ten, they don't have surveillance. And sometimes, surveillance is what keeps people honest.

As she parked, she picked up her phone and dialed TK. He answered on the third ring. "I'm outside," she told him.

"A'ight. Go ahead and come in." Ty got out and made her way to the door. She tried to memorize her surroundings. Just in case she had to make a trip back for whatever reason.

TK answered the door in a pair of black shorts, no shirt and a blunt in his mouth. "Come in." As Ty walked through the house, she could tell it was as advertised. *A trap house.*

There was one couch, a TV and a table to bust dope down on. Ty took a seat as TK left to go get her a drink. "What's up, baby girl?" TK's homeboy—Osama—came from the back of the house. He was also in shorts, but had a black wife beater on. Both of them couldn't be any older than 21. "You smoke?" Osama asked.

"Sometimes. What y'all smoking on?'

"This right here is Girl Scout Cookie." Osama passed her the blunt. Ty took a big pull and held it until her lungs exploded.

"*Awka! Awka!*" She began to choke, feeling her whole body tingling. TK came from the back with a cup of Hennessy for her and a plate covered with powder for him.

"You fuck around?" he asked, gesturing to the plate.

"Oh naw. I don't snort. I just smoke weed, pop pills and drink liquor," Ty told him.

"Well. You don't mind if I do, do you?"

Ty shrugged. "That's your bidness." TK didn't hesitate to snort up four big lines. Two in each nostril. Thirty minutes of chilling and drugging, Ty figured it was time to get the ball rolling. "So . . . Who's first?" TK leaned back, dug his hand in his shorts, and pulled out his dick. Ty was surprised and disappointed to see it was still flaccid. "Money, first baby." Osama reached over and handed her the money. She counted it, then placed it in her bra. She grabbed his dick, wet her lips, stretched her jaw and dove right in. Ty pulled on his cock with her mouth, stretching it to its limits, while massaging his nuts.

Spit trickled down his shaft, saturating his balls. After fifteen minutes, TK was still flaccid. This was the first time that ever happened to Ty. Period! She tried every trick she learned over the years. Still, nothing! After twenty minutes, she decided to move on to Osama. "Look, TK. Let me handle your boy, and I'll come back to you. Obviously, it's the dope. Just let it wear off a little bit." Reluctantly, TK allowed her to switch.

He watched as she got Osama rock-hard in seconds. They slipped the condom on him. In no time, he was hitting Ty from the back. Her skirt was flipped up and bunched around her waists. Ass cheeks jiggling, as he gutted her out, her pussy began to fart. She came while pounding her fist into the carpet. "Ohhh, fuck. Shit!" she cried. "I'm cumming. Oh my Gawd, I'm cummmmi-innnggg!"

Ty had to admit. The young nigga had some good stroke game. She looked down at TK's dick and saw it was still on wet noodle status. She decided to enjoy a little more of Osama's good dick.

The next hour was spent with Osama fucking her in multiple positions. She laid on his chest, while making her ass bounce up and down cock. With a growl, Osama filled the condom up. His second nut of the night.

After he peeled the rubber off, he excused himself. Ty focused her attention back on TK. She glanced at her watch. With thirty minutes left to go, he'd better get his shit together. Or, he would be shit out of luck. Once again, Ty stuffed him into her mouth.

Sucking deeply on the head, she cuffed his balls and played with them. In hopes, he would rise to the occasion. Thirty minutes later. Still, nothing. Frustrated, she popped him out of her mouth. "Look, TK. I gotta go. I can't be here all night."

TK frowned. "What you mean you gotta go? I ain't even got my nut yet."

"Okay. But that ain't my fault. I did what I had to do," she argued.

"Well. Give me my money back then."

Now, it was Ty's turn to frown. "Give you what? Boy, stop playing with me. I put my mouth on you. That money's mine." Ty got up to leave. TK grabbed her arm.

"Bitch. You ain't going nowhere. Not until I get my nut, or I get my bread back."

Ty snatched her arm back. "Say, man, don't touch me." Ty rushed to the front door. She felt something was about to go down. She eased her hand in her purse and took a hold of her box cutter. As soon as she stepped outside, she felt the blow to her right ear. Ty stumbled and fell into the grass.

"Bitch. You got me all types of fucked up, if you think you're leaving with my money," TK yelled furiously. He stood over her, face twisted in rage. Ty slowly began to rise. Still dazed from the surprise attack. She gripped the box cutter tightly, concealing it in her purse.

As soon as TK grabbed ahold of her hair, forcing her to stand up, Ty swung wildly. She aimed for his neck. But instead, she opened up the side of his face. "Awww, fuck!"

He screamed in surprise and agony. The box cutter separated his nose in two.

Blood instantly gushed forth. TK grabbed his face, twisting and writhing in pain. Something inside her clicked. Ty felt a deep desire to finish the job, slit his throat and leave him there to water the grass. But, her better judgment won.

She hurried off to the car, put it in drive and fled the scene. As she pulled up to the room, she broke down and cried. She wasn't sure she could continue doing what she needed to do, without the proper protection. Ty really didn't give a damn about the danger, per se, but she couldn't afford anything to happen to her before she accomplished her goal.

Ty needed to make things right for Bo and the kids. As she sat in the car, she saw the same young nigga from a few weeks back. Ty studied him for a second. He was tall, well-built and had an edge to him. She wondered, would he be willing to assist her? How would she be able to assist him? It was obvious he needed money, since he was staying at the motel also. Maybe, she could work out some type of percentage to give him.

He walked towards the lobby's entrance. As he returned back to his room, she hopped out of the car. He jumped back at her sudden appearance. "Oh. My bad. I didn't mean to scare you," she offered.

"Naw, you good. You just sort of surprised me. I didn't think no one was in the car," he told her honestly.

"Yeah. I was just sitting here thinking. But anyway, would you happen to know where I could find some weed?"

Marcus looked at her suspiciously. "You ain't *Twelve*, is you?"

"Police?" Ty snorted. "Naw, baby, I'm the furthest thing from a pig. I stay a couple doors down from you."

He thought about it. Then, it dawned on him. "Oh yeah, that's right. You got kids with you."

"Yup. That's me. So, you got some weed on you?"

"Yeah, I got some." He turned around and headed into his room. " Come in." Ty followed Marcus into the room and was pleasantly surprised.

*He must have been staying here for a while,* she surmised. He and the tiny room looking like it belonged in a middle class home. "What you trynna spend?"

"How much are your grams?"

"Well, I do G's for $20. For you, I'll do $10."

A small smile formed on Ty's face. "Why the discount?"

"For one, you're my neighbor. For two, you look like you need it." Ty's smile got even brighter.

"Well. In that case, give me a 8."

"Just shoot me $25 then." Ty paid him. He weighed her a three point five, bagged it up, and then handed it to her.

"You wanna smoke one?" she asked, looking for a reason to spend more time with him.

"I ain't tripping. Matter of fact, I'll match you." Ty twisted up a blunt. They blew hers first, then back door and blew his. Even though he seemed nice enough, Ty could tell Marcus was a little slow. Sometimes, he would space out in the middle of a conversation. Other times, he would mince up his words when he became excited.

Once Ty heard his life story, she understood fully.

Having the drugs in his system at birth affected him. As they talked, she would sometimes pry her legs apart, to give him a peek. She felt assured of his sexual preference, but still wanted to make sure. Based on the tent forming in the front of his shorts, she could tell he at least liked pussy.

A part of her felt bad about manipulating him, but fuck it. She needed a warm, strong body to protect her. Ty spent the rest of the night getting in Marcus's head. She knew, whenever she finally did give him the pussy, he would be head over heels. She needed him completely and utterly invested in her. Time was not on her side. Every day counted.

Her joints were constantly inflamed. Her bones hurt. Some nights, her nerves felt raw. It was hard for her to sleep on a regular mattress, she needed one filled with air.

When she finally left his room, it was 5:38 a.m. She felt confident he would be hers to mold. She walked into her room and felt at ease. Even though her situation hadn't changed, per se, something about Marcus being in her life felt right. He felt safe and secured.

Both the kids were sound asleep. She noticed snack wrappers laying around. No doubt, they were enjoying their dietary freedom. Ty reached under the bed, and grabbed her stash. She added $920. After filling the tank up, grabbing something to eat and buying the weed, that's what she had left.

Ty jumped in the shower, to wash away the day. She looked down. Blood poured into the drain. TK's blood stained her hands. She learned something about herself. She could hurt someone and not feel the least bit bad about it.

## 13

TWO WEEKS LATER. At approximately 2:30 a.m., Ty was pushing it down I-10, headed back to the Eastside. In the passenger seat, draped in all-black, with a smoking gun in his lap was Marcus. They'd just left the house of a known drug dealer in Katy, named Drop.

Ty had met Drop at an upscale lounge downtown called Prosper. Since she was the baddest thing in there that night, to Drop, it was a no-brainer.

He was your typical flashy dope dealer. He loved to show off his money and never hesitated to put his business out there. It didn't take Ty long to figure out, he kept his stash at his house in Katy.

Five days after meeting Drop, Ty was on Fry Road at said house. Laying on the couch, watching HULU. Drop rubbing on her feet. Since he was twenty-five, he took pride in bagging an older, sophisticated, thoroughbred chick like Ty.

She'd convinced him that she knew all the movers and

shakers in the dope game. And if he stuck with her, she'd make sure he leveled up and became the next King of the City. Ty was supposed to be spending the night. As soon as she got to his crib, she wasted no time pouncing on him.

Of course, Drop could never resist her. The only problem was, they had dinner reservations they were sure to miss. After a quick movie, and a round of hot and steamy sex, Drop elected to hop in the shower and get cleaned up. Even though they'd missed their dinner reservations, he still wanted to hit the town. He never passed up an opportunity to show the city the type of bitch he had on his arm.

As Drop showered, Ty let Marcus in through the back-door. Drop emerged from the bathroom, cheerful. Then, everything went black.

'SMACK!' "Wake up!" Drop felt the sharp sting to his face. He struggled to shake the cobwebs loose. He couldn't move. He looked down and realized he was strapped to a chair. Blood trickled down the side of his face. A deep gash throbbed above his right eyebrow. Once his vision came back into focus, he couldn't believe what he saw.

Standing before him was Ty. She had some nigga with a hammer, standing next to her. "Bitch! This how you do a nigga? After all the love I showed you."

Ty's face tightened. "Love? Nigga, you joking, right? First of all, you've got to be one of the dumbest niggas in the dope game. You ain't know a bitch thirty seconds, and I'm all in your crib. I know *all* of your bidness. Truthfully, I'm surprised niggas ain't been got your ass," Ty spat.

Drop really couldn't say shit to contest that. He'd been fooled. He was really feeling Ty, and would have made her his wifey. Now, he wasn't sure what type of timing she was on. Drop couldn't look at her. So, he looked at the nigga instead. Marcus remained stone-faced.

Him and Ty had agreed, she would do all the talking. "What's the combination to the safe?" Ty asked.

"Bitch. Fuck you," Drop spat.

"Oh yeah? Fuck me? Fuck me. A'ight." Ty nodded towards Marcus. Marcus took one step, swung and shattered four of Drops' front teeth with the hammer.

"Agghhh," Drop screamed. Mouth wide, teeth half broken. Gums swollen and bloody. Pieces of his teeth ricocheted off the back of his throat, which he swallowed involuntarily. Drop shook, struggled, then began to cry.

Realization dawned on him. He may die. The only chance he had was to give up the money. "Do you still wanna fuck me? Huh?" Ty prodded.

Drop shook his head. Blood poured from his broken mouth. "Okay. Okay. Imma gi dit tu yuh." They could barely understand what he was saying. Marcus brought a pad and pen. They told him to write down the combination.

Once they had it, Ty opened the safe up. Her eyes lit up. It looked like Drop had about $30,000 and what appeared to be a half a brick of cocaine. Even though that wasn't a lot of money in the streets, to Ty, it was a small fortune. That was the most she had ever seen at one time. "Grab a pillowcase," she told Marcus.

He didn't hesitate. As Marcus stuffed the pillow case with the money and dope, Ty turned towards Drop. His eyes pleaded for mercy. "Look, Drop. This wasn't personal. I hope next time you learn from your mistakes." She walked off, after giving Marcus a look. Drop heard the words "next time" and felt a rush of relief. She was going to let him make it. *Or, so he thought.*

As soon as Ty left the room, Marcus grabbed the uncovered pillow, shoved it against Drop's head. The chair tipped and fell over backwards. Still strapped to the chair, Drop couldn't move. Only scream. But even those were muffled by the pillow. Marcus pressed down and grabbed the gun off his waists. He pointed it, at the exact same location Drop's forehead should be, and squeezed. *'Bocka!'*

Drop's head bounced off the carpet. Marcus could smell the blood, gunpowder and singed cotton. Drop's brains pooled around his head like a bonnet. Marcus stared at the lifeless body. His second kill. He knew it would not be his last.

As they drove in silence, an unspoken bond had been forged between them. They now shared a secret they would need to take to their graves. Only difference: Ty's projected time on earth was a lot shorter than Marcus's. Of course, she had yet to tell him this. Marcus's loyalty stemmed from his growing affection for her. He'd fallen head over heels, in that short amount of time.

Once they got back to the motel, they retreated back to Marcus's room. They didn't want to wake the kids. Ty poured the money and drugs onto the bed. "Twist up a blunt. I'll count the money up," she told him as she undressed. Down to her bra and panties. She knew Marcus wouldn't be able to keep his eyes off of her. Which would make things a lot easier.

Ty sat Indian-style. Her back against the headboard. Her panties were jacked into her slit. Her sex lips were exposed, popping out the side of the crotch band. The money sat in a pile. Marcus twisted up a blunt and was puffing on it. Playing on his phone, while peeking at Ty's love box, every chance he got.

She counted up and separated into two piles. "It came out to be $22,680," she claimed. Actually, the count was $31,280. She manipulated the stacks to look the same in height and bills, but her stack contained higher denominations. While Marcus had a lil over $11,000, Ty made out with over twenty bands.

"What about the drugs?" he asked, happy to get his cut.

"I'm about to call someone up, who's in the game. I'ma see what he'll give me for it," she told him.

"A'ight. Well, let me know." Marcus stripped down to his boxers and went to take a shower. As soon as he was gone, she pulled out her phone and called Pat.

"Hello," he answered. He sounded as if he may have been on the way to sleep.

"Wassup? Say, I just came across something you might wanna grab."

"Oh yeah? What is it?"

"I don't wanna talk about it over the phone. Can we meet up somewhere?" Pat looked over at his wife asleep. He'd been wanting to catch up with Ty, ever since he saw her. That's why, after he dropped Meme off, he doubled back and scooped up Ty's number. Up until then, he hadn't had a chance to slide up in her guts.

"Meet me at the Scottish Inn, on I-10 and Normandy," he whispered as he crept out of bed."

"I'm on the way now." After she hung up the phone, Ty grabbed her cut, the half a brick and texted Marcus to let him know she was meeting up with a potential buyer.

She went back to her room and took a quick wash off. After scrubbing her coochie, her armpits and her ass crack, she stashed the money under the mattress, kissed the kids as they slept, then walked back out the door.

Ty pulled up to the Scottish Inn, thinking she was early. Pat was already there waiting on her. He texted her and let her know he'd gotten them a room. *"So they could talk in private"*

She already knew Pat was fiending for some of her goodies. Ty purposely kept him at bay. Ty grabbed the bag with the dope in it, hopped out the car and made her way to the room. As she stepped inside, she wasted no time. "Look. Before I show you what I got, I want you to know. I'm a street bitch. I've been around hustlers my whole life. So, please, don't think you'll be able to fuck over me." She pointed her finger at him, to further drive home her point.

"Come on, Ty. What I look like fucking over you? I ain't no crumb, bum ass nigga. I stand on bidness, and pack fair with *whoever* I'm dealing with," Pat assured her.

"A'ight. Well, what you gone give me for this?" Ty reached in her bag and pulled out the brick of hard dope and handed it to him. Pat grabbed it, smelled it and analyzed it.

"Well. Right now, a whole thing is going for $28-$30 . . . $26 at the lowest. Just on the strength that it's you, I'll give you $15 for the half. Ty was pleasantly surprised. She really thought he would low ball her and try to give her $8-$10 for it.

"That's a bet!"

"Okay, but I don't have the bread on me. I can take it with me and bring the money back," Pat told her.

"How long will that take?"

"Not long. I stay ten minutes away. In the New Forest subdivision. I just have to run to the house and grab it real quick and I'll be back."

Ty really didn't want to let him leave with it, but she didn't want to keep riding around with it either. Plus, in his defense, she didn't tell him what she had. So, he didn't know to bring any money. She began to undress. Pat's jaw dropped. "What you doing?"

"Shit. If you 'bout to be gone, I'ma get comfortable, and wait for you to come back," she teased. Ty knew Pat wanted her in the worst way. She felt, if he had something to come back to, that would decrease the chances of him burning her.

Ty sat on the bed. Back against the headboard. She pulled her knees up. Her feet were flat on the bed, causing her coochie to pop out at him. Pat's dick jumped for joy. He subconsciously licked his lips, staring at her enormous camel toe. "Soooo. You gone go or what?" Pat hadn't even realized that he was stuck staring.

He snapped out of his trance. "Yeah, yeah. Let me go," he stammered. While he was gone, Ty got a text from Marcus.

Marcus: *U good?*

Ty: *Yeah. My people say they gone grab it for 10 bands. So that's 5 apiece.*

Marcus: *Cool. LMK when u get back.*

Ty: *Will do.*

. . .

Ty knew she was wrong for cheating her little friend. But in her eyes, she needed it more than him. Plus, he seemed content with his share of things. As long as he's happy, she didn't see any real problem.

Thirty minutes later, Pat returned with 15k. Ty was still half naked as she counted the money, before she placed it in her purse. She looked Pat up and down. She had half a mind, to leave him with a hard dick and blue balls. She thought about something he said, and felt the time was right to put the pussy on him.

Pat stood transfixed from her beauty. You couldn't tell Ty was sick, just by looking at her. She still had her weight. Her disease wasn't necessarily one that affected her externally. Little did anyone know, Lupus aka the *wolf disease*, was eating up her insides.

"Come here," she mouthed. Her legs splayed wide open. Pat unbuckled his Fendi belt and allowed his pants to drop to the floor. He damn near ripped his shirt off, trying to get it off of him. He'd been dreaming about Ty's pussy for the last couple days.

He didn't know what it was about her that drove him crazy, but he had to have her. He crawled in bed, stuffed his nose between her crease and inhaled deeply. Her scent made his dick jump. He loved a woman who kept her snatch fresh.

Ty reached down, grabbed ahold of his head and pulled him even deeper into her box. "Eat it up for me, baby. Let me flood your mouth with this cum," she purred.

Pat began to lick between her folds. Lapping up her sweet tasty secretions. She began to work her hips. He pulled the hood of her clit back, exposing her jelly bean nub. He swiped the tip of his tongue across the top. Her body began to spasm. "Oooh, ssshit! That's it, Pat. Suck on that pussy, baby," she urged. Pat obliged, trapping her clit between his lips. He sucked and swiped, then sucked and swiped, until she went into convulsions. He pushed two fingers into her cunt, massaging the sponge-like skin at the roof of her pussy. Ty's eyes rolled back. Her nut began to bubble. "Oh shit. Oh shit. Here it cums. Oh my Gawd, I'm cumming. I'm cumming I'm cumming. Fuuucckkk!" She squeezed his ears and hung on for dear life. Her cum spewed into his mouth, splashing against his lips in the process.

Pat could smell and taste her peach-flavored essence. He continued to hungrily lap at her folds, sopping up the excess liquid. As Ty sat paralyzed, trembling from a devastating orgasm, Pat crawled up her body. Spreading her legs wider, in order to receive him, Ty looked down between them, watching, as Pat strapped on the Magnum. Seconds later, he split her opening.

Her back arched. Her fingers clawed at him as his dick bottomed out. "Fuck!" He growled. "Your shit wet as a motherfucka." He began to pop his hips, as he sawed into her. '*Squish. Squish. Squish.*' The sound of wet noodles being stirred is all that could be heard, as Pat fucked Ty into the worn-out mattress.

Before he knew it, his balls began to burst. "Awww, fuuuccck. I'm 'bout to nut!" He hopped out of her pussy, snatched the condom off. Ty opened her mouth up. "Ahhhhh, ssshit!" Pat threw his head back and unloaded, painting her face with his hot milky cream.

. . .

Ty didn't make it back until well after 6 in the morning. She
was parked. Just staring at Marcus's room door. She wanted
to knock, but she figured he would be asleep. Instead, she
headed to her own room. She decided she'd just give him
his cut in the morning.

As soon as she was about to unlock her room door, she
heard the sound of his opening. The look Marcus had on his
face made her feel some type of way. She knew he looked
at them as a couple. After all, she needed him to believe
that, in order to go as hard as he was going for her and her
kids.

But now, she was starting to feel bad about certain
things. He had cemented the ultimate act of loyalty . . .
Murder. Now that she had it, she felt the weight and the
burden.

Ty had just lied and cheated him out of his money
twice. Not to mention, she just let a nigga run up in her and
cum all over her face. Marcus looked tired. Ty could tell
he'd been up all night worried. He was mature enough not
to blow her phone up. For that, she gave him major points.

She approached him timidly. "Here goes your cut." Ty
held out the money. Marcus looked at it, then her. Finally,
he took it from her. "Well. I'm tired, babe, so . . ."

"Are you spending the night?" Since they had been
messing around, Ty would often spend the night in his
room. She didn't feel right about it now.

"Naw, babe. Imma crash with the kids. I'll come over in
the morning and we can go grab something to eat." Marcus
was clearly disappointed, but she shrugged it off.

"Okay. Well, I'll see you tomorrow." He turned and
headed back inside, leaving Ty alone on the sidewalk.

Once he stepped inside, he didn't even bother to count the money. He just stashed it under his dresser. He was hurt; Ty didn't want to spend the night with him. He didn't know what it was, but he was almost certain he was madly in love with her. He just hoped that she would one day feel the same way about him.

He was still looking over his shoulder, dealing with the Trey situation. Now, he had the Drop play to worry about. Yet, each one of those bodies he felt had been necessary. If he had to do it again, he wouldn't hesitate. Especially, if it had anything to do with Ty. Marcus laid back with his eyes closed. Soon, he was fast asleep, dreaming about his possible future with the woman that he loved.

**14**

It's 7:30 a.m. Bo's sitting in the day room watching Sports Center. Drinking a cup of coffee. His money from the county hadn't hit his account yet, but Brown Sugar had put some money on his books. He was able to go to store and get what he needed.

Bo liked to hit the day room early in the morning. Most people were at work or at school at that time, so the day room would be almost empty. "Excuse me. Do you be messing with them cakes?" Bo looked up. A thin, brown-skinned man by the name of Rose, was staring down at him.

Rose was 5'10", 155 lbs. The waves on his head were spinning in what they called "the wrap" pattern. He had tattooed eyebrows, and often wore Kool Aid over his lips and cheeks. He'd been locked up 6 years on a 20-year sentence. And at 25 years old, he was looking for a man. "Uhh. What all you got on it?" Bo had a sweet tooth. A piece of cake would definitely hit the spot.

"It's pumpkin spice. With chico sticks, M&M's and cream cheese pound cake," Rose pitched.

"How much?"

"I usually charge a dollar fifty a slice, but since you're a new customer, I'll give you one to try. If you like it, which I know you will, then you can pull back up and shop with me." Rose felt confident in his product.

"A'ight. Well, let me see what you're working with." Rose ran off to retrieve the piece of cake. Bo bit into it and had to admit, it was definitely worth a dollar fifty. He quickly flagged Rose down for another slice. This time, Rose sparked up a conversation.

"So. Your name's Bo, right?"

"Yeah. What's yours?"

"Rose. Where you from?"

"I'm from Houston. What about you?"

"I'm from Dallas. Oak Cliff. Tripp Trippp," Rose responded with a smile. "You gotta a lot of time, Bo?"

Bo took a deep breath. It was still hard for him to voice it. It seemed like each time he did, it meant he was accepting it. "Yeah. I got a life sentence."

"Damn. That's fucked up. I got six done on a twenty myself. You mind if I sit wit' you?"

"Shit. Do you." Rose went ahead and sat down. The two of them talked about their families, their cases and their situations with Krash.

"Why did you and Krash get into it?" Rose fished.

"The nigga tried to salt me down, so I had to check that shit." Rose wanted him to elaborate more, so he could check Bo's temperature.

"What he say? If you don't mind me asking?" Bo got

silent for a minute. Trying to decide if he should go down that road with Rose.

"A'ight. So look, I got a homeboy I met in the county named Brown Sugar." Rose's eyebrows rose after hearing the name. "When we were in the county, I used to look out for him. Make sure nobody messed with him and he used to shoot me bread. Well, he came to see me. I guess Krash was down there at visit, came back and told people I was down there on some extra shit."

Rose didn't want to push too soon, but he had to ask. "What you mean, on some extra shit? I'm kind of lost."

"Look. Brown Sugar is one of yours. Krash was trying to say we was down there kissing, on more shit. I fuck with Brown Sugar the long way, but wasn't none of that shit going down. So, when I found out, I pulled up on him." Rose wanted to ask more, but left the subject alone.

"Get ready for Chow!" Bo looked at his watch. Him and Rose had been chopping it up for two and a half hours. They both decided they were going to go eat.

Bo went to grab the dollar fifty for Rose. When he pulled up on his cell, Rose was out of uniform, sitting on the bed in some custom made boxers. They were way too small. Bo handed him the meat pack and was about to leave. "Hold on a second. Can I ask you something?" Rose questioned.

"Wassup?" Bo kind of felt he already knew what Rose needed to ask him. It was like deja vu.

"Well. I was wondering if you'd be interested in partaking in the same type of agreement you had with your friend Brown Sugar. But, with me. You know, it's hard for a bitch like me to make it in a place like this. I'll pay you every store, just to hold me down. To make sure nobody tries to take advantage of me."

Bo was speechless. He didn't understand what about him that was attracting these individuals. Before catching the case, he hadn't so much as spoken to a homosexual man. Now, he had two of them who'd proposition him. Get paid for protection.

Rose saw the hesitation, and upped the ante. "Plus, I got a lil motion on the contraband. So, whatever I get, I'll give it all to you."

Bo nodded, before verbally committing. "That's a bet. Come out at last chow so we can chop it up."

"You going to lunch?" Rose asked.

"I was, but . . ."

"Naw. Don't go. I'll fix you a bowl. Matter fact, you don't ever have to go to chow. I'll make sure you have a bowl whenever you're hungry," Rose assured him.

Bo shrugged. "A'ight. Fuck it." He headed back to his cell. Bo knew he was playing a dangerous game. Nothing came for free. He wondered what price he'd have to pay for the perks Rose was offering.

———

Corey checked the time once again. "Shit!" He cursed under his breath. He didn't want to deal with his baby momma today, but he had a scheduled *surprise* visit with his boys. He couldn't miss it. This was the first time he would see them, since the murder. He was barely able to spend time with them beforehand.

Kourtney was one of those females that felt, if you

didn't want to be with her, then you didn't want to be with her kids. Him and Kourtney had two boys together. Cajun and Karver. Cajun looked just like him. Karver, on the other hand, resembled Kourtney more than anything else. It'd been plenty of times Corey questioned if Karver was his. He intended on taking a blood test, but was trying to find a way to do it without Kourtney finding out. If she ever did discover he had a blood test administered, she'd go slap the fuck off. His visit was scheduled from 1:00 p.m. to 3:00 p.m. It was already 1:20. No doubt, he was going to hear her mouth.

Corey pulled into her apartment complex. There was a group of people standing around, smoking and kicking the shit. Nobody looked to be over 20 years old. The youngest, maybe 15. Corey recognized one of the older ones. A little rowdy nigga by the name of Rah Rah.

Rah was 19 and fresh home from TYC. His light skin and curly hair would give you the impression he was soft. Wrong! Rah was increasingly gaining a reputation as a steppa. He had a lot to learn before he could make a claim for the title of Boss, but he showed he had lots of potential.

Corey parked his pearl white Cadillac DTS on 84's. He was happy as hell, he finally got his *baby* out of the shop. Even though the car was more than 20 years old, Corey kept it in pristine shape. He did the foreign whips already. Now, it was back to American made.

Rah saw Corey, and his face lit up. He idolized Corey. Corey and Kourtney had been messing around, almost as long as Rah had been alive. When Rah was 6-7 years old, Corey used to pull up and buy him cool cups, nachos and candy. "What's popping, big homie?" Rah greeted.

Corey shook him up and gave him a one-handed homie hug. "You know me, lil bro, getting to that bag. What y'all smoking on?" Rah looked embarrassed.

"Man. Ain't shit but some reggie," Rah confessed. Corey went back to his car, grabbed a sack of Guerilla Glue and two cigarillos. He tossed them to him.

"Twist one up for y'all, and hold the other one for me. I'm 'bout to go kick it with my kids. When I get back, we'll blow," he told him.

"Fa shit sho. I got you," Rah assured him excitedly. He couldn't believe it. He was about to smoke with the big homie. Before Corey parted ways, he noticed a brown-skinned female staring a hole into him.

He didn't know who she was, but could tell she was young. Plus, the way she hovered over Rah's shoulder, Corey guessed she must've been his girlfriend.

Corey tried not to stare, but her booty shorts were all up in her gap. Her perky C cups were sitting up. Corey could tell she didn't have a bra on. He couldn't help but wonder, did she have some good pussy?

He shook it off and continued towards his baby momma's apartment. He didn't look back, but could feel the young chick's eyes following him.

Corey walked up the stairs and approached Kourtney's door. She could be heard screaming for the boys to "sit yall's asses down!" *Knock! Knock! Knock!* The door swung open. Corey expected to be greeted by an angry baby momma. Instead, he got an irritating and instigating best friend. Liz!

Liz and Kourtney had been best friends their whole lives. Liz was a slim, light-skinned woman, with a big mouth and a very nasty attitude toward him. Corey didn't understand where all the animosity was coming from. For some reason, Liz couldn't stand him. The feeling was mutual. "Kourtney. Your whack ass baby daddy's here," Liz hollered over her shoulder.

"Whack? Come on, Liz. You would shoot yourself in the foot to be my baby momma."

"Psssht . . . Nigga, please. You ain't good for shit, but giving a bitch an STI. I don't know why Kourtney deals with your sorry ass. You don't even take care of your kids," she shot at him.

Corey gritted his teeth. The last thing he wanted to do was go upside Liz's head. That would surely get his visitation rights revoked. He had to be the bigger man. "Can you *please* step aside, so I can visit my sons?"

"Pssht. Whateva, nigga." Liz stepped aside. The boys were sitting on the couch. When they saw their father, they exploded. "Daddy! Daddy! Daddy!" Corey's face lit up. He scooped them up in a great big bear hug.

The rest of the visit was spent with him playing with the boys. Kourtney barely said much the whole time. But, as soon as Corey was getting ready to leave, she decided to act as if she cared. "So. Damn! You not gone even give a bitch a hug?" Corey still had love for his baby momma. It's just, she could be extra sometimes. He turned around and gave her what she wanted. *A hug.*

She purred in his ear, when she felt his dick pressed against her mound. Kourtney was a bad bitch. "Redbone. 38-inch ass. Thick thighs, with some juicy lips. Her coochie was always wet. If they hadn't separated, she might have had two more little rug rats running around. Her cat was too good to pull out of. "When you gone come home, Corey?" she whispered.

"I don't know, Kourt. You gotta chill out with all that insecure shit. Every time I turn around, you accusing me of fucking the next bitch."

Kourtney wanted to say, *"That's because you are."* Instead, she said "Well. I'm sorry, but you know how crazy I am about that slab of dick you carry around. Plus, I know them hoes are scandalous as fuck." Kourtney loved Corey with every fiber. Even after he burned her twice.

He was a serial cheater. But, she only caught him once. Well, technically, she didn't catch him. She walked in, and the house smelled like sex. Corey was in the bathroom, and her little cousin was watching TV. Soon after, Corey had given her the Clap.

Corey squeezed on her ass cheeks. Liz smacked her lips at the public display of affection. Corey broke the embrace. "I'll holla at you, when your pet monkey ain't around."

"Uh-Uh. Don't do me, nigga," Liz called out as Corey walked out and shut the door behind him. He could still hear her ranting, as he traveled down the stairs. He honestly didn't expect Rah Rah to be waiting, but there he was. Unlit blunt in his hand.

He saw the expression on Corey's face and offered him to spark the blunt. After lighting it, Corey hit it twice and immediately began to relax. His mind began to drift. He thought about how soft Kourtney's ass had been.

Instinctively, he glanced between the young chick's thighs. Her camel toe was looking meaty. Corey wet his lips. He looked up and caught her staring. An unspoken conversation was being conducted with their eyes.

Meanwhile, Rah was going on about his plans to come up and how he was destined to take over the streets.

The more Corey observed the young chick, the more he wanted her. He just didn't know how he could make it happen. Apparently, she did. "Baby. Can I have some money? I'm 'bout to walk to the store."

Rah was only slightly annoyed by her interruption. He was aware that his big homie was present, and he didn't want to appear like a bum ass nigga. He pulled his knot out and peeled off a hundred-dollar bill. "Here, babe." The chick grabbed it, and stuffed it in her back pocket. She pulled the shorts out her ass, as she made her way down the street, towards the store.

Corey watched her ass move and sway. He almost followed her right then and there. He had to play it smart though. He waited about five minutes, before he bid farewell to the group. Corey made sure he drove in the opposition direction, from where the young chick was walking towards.

It didn't really matter. He was able to go through the neighborhood, come out on Wallisville and be at the store in less than three minutes. He cruised the parking lot. Looking. Searching. She stood on the sidewalk, hoping. Praying. Waiting!

Corey pulled up to the sidewalk and popped the door open. "Get in." She hurriedly hopped in. He drove off, checking the rearview mirror. "What's your name, lil momma?"

"Porsche."

"How old are you?"

"I'm nineteen," she told him.

"You sure 'bout that?"

"You wanna see my ID?" she said indignantly.

Corey gave her a side eyed glance. "You and Rah go together?" She looked uncomfortable answering the question. She didn't expect Corey to ask her those types of questions. Honestly, she didn't know what to expect.

"Yeah. We've been talking for like seven months," she admitted. Corey made a right into the subdivision, Pine Trails. It was the only neighborhood on the East that had alleys behind the houses. He found the street he was looking for, and took the alleyway.

"Do you love him?" Corey asked while pulling into a driveway.

"I mean. I care for him," she said tentatively. Corey leaned his seat back, cut the engine off and reached for his buckled belt. Porsche's heart quickened. She stared intently, as Corey reached into his boxers with his left hand.

With his right, he grabbed the back of her head. With little hesitation, Porsche's head fell into Corey's lap. His warm dick slid between her wet lips. "Ssshhittt. Suck that dick," Corey urged her as he pumped in and out of her mouth. He closed his eyes and pictured Kourtney's pretty pink pussy. "Fuck! I'm 'bout to cum. Swallow the dick, you dirty lil bitch."

Corey pushed her head down, bucked and unloaded. Porsche's mouth flooded with cum. She jerked once, then gulped down each load, moaning, as cum drizzled down her throat. "Aww! Aww, shit!" Corey panted. Porsche pulled back, allowing his dick to flop free.

He looked at her, reached over and scooped a drop of cum that hung at the corner of her mouth. He held it out for her. She accepted the offering, sucking on his finger until it was clean as a whistle.

As they headed home, Porsche asked if he could take her to get something to eat. For her and Rah. Corey did, but he also made her buy him something to eat also. Even though he had a pocket full of money.

He dropped her down the street from the apartments. "Tell my lil homie to get at me," he said as Porsche hopped out the car. She pulled her shorts out the crack of her ass and from between her pussy crack.

"Okay, I will." With that, she headed back down the street. Where her boyfriend was waiting for her. Corey headed back to the spot. Not a guilty bone in his body.

# 15

MEME WAS LAYING IN BED. Sweaty and sticky from another round of steamy sex with Pat. They'd been going strong for the last couple of weeks. She still considered Slick to be her boyfriend, but she would often tell people Pat was her man. She had feelings for Slick, but Pat's money was longer. So. When he called, she came running.

She watched Pat slink out of bed, headed to the restroom. Meme had to admit to herself, he was one fine piece of dark chocolate. She felt as though she'd hit the lotto. As the shower began to run, his phone began to ring. Normally, she wouldn't dare invade his privacy. Something told her to see who was calling.

Meme grabbed his phone and was shocked to see Ty's number flash against the screen. She became furious. Now that she had found her ideal man, Ty had the audacity to try and steal him from right under her nose. Meme's blood began to boil. She couldn't charge Pat up about it. Because technically, they weren't a couple. Pat already made it clear, he wanted drama-free sex. Meme decided to text the number back.

Pat: *My bad. I couldn't answer, but wassup?*

Ty: *r u still trynna get 2gether 2morrow?*

Meme didn't want to set off any alarms, but she needed to find out how close the two of them were. She responded how she thought Pat would.

Pat: *You already know I'm trynna link up. U gone let a nigga taste some of that?*

Ty: *U ain't full from last time?*

Meme cringed. She was genuinely hurt.

Pat: *A nigga like me gots a big appetite. Plus, that seems like 4ever ago.*

Ty: *Boy. That was last week. But I got you.*

Meme concluded the conversation, then deleted the thread. Now she knew Ty was fucking her man. No doubt, trying to get her back for fucking on Corey. Meme told herself she would keep her emotions in check. She couldn't risk getting beside herself and possibly running Pat into the next bitch's arms. She knew one thing for sure, she needed to get Ty out of the picture. For good!

Black N Mild was an older cat, who'd been hustling under the radar for quite some time. At 5'9", 160 lbs, with skin the color of boot leather, he really wasn't an opposing figure. But when it came to getting a bag, he was a demon.

Ty met him at the Shell off Federal Road one night. Right after she'd gotten done messing with Pat. After her and Black N Mild exchanged numbers, they hooked up a few times.

One night, after he'd dropped Ty off, Marcus followed him back to the spot he laid his head at. That was five days ago. Through his surveillance, Marcus learned that Black N Mild stayed with his baby momma and their young daughter, who was still a toddler.

After relaying that information to Ty, they devised a plan. As Black N Mild laid fast asleep, courtesy of some bomb ass head and a cocktail of crushed up OxyContin and four bars, Ty took his house keys to a locksmith to get copied. That was yesterday.

Now, he was once again at a hotel, knee-deep between Ty's thighs. Marcus walked into his house, unmolested. Black N Mild's family slept in the master bedroom. When he returned at 2 a.m., he was ambushed walking into his own home. Now, he was tied up. His baby momma in her panties. No bra, zipped tied. Then, there was a nigga he'd never seen before, sitting on the bed next to her, caressing a hunting knife.

Black N Mild immediately started to plead. "Look, dawg. I don't know what you want, but please, man. Don't hurt my family." His baby momma—Corra—began screaming into the duct tape. Tears streamed down her face. Her infant daughter must have sensed the impending danger, because she began to wail.

Marcus allowed him to think the worst. "Where's the money?"

Black N Mild shook his head. "I don't have any money," he said.

"Oh, you think this a game?" Marcus took the hunting knife and ran the edge of the blade down Corra's face, splitting her cheek in half, like a fresh apple. She screamed in agony. Her blood gushed from the wound. Black N Mild shut his eyes tightly, trying to will the image away. Even with his eyes closed, he could still hear Corra screaming while his daughter continued to ball. When he finally found the courage to open them, Marcus held his daughter in his arms. "Oh, no, no, no. Please, man. She's just a child." Marcus grabbed the blood stained knife and rotated the blade.

"I bet your daughter won't be able to take it as well as your baby momma did. What do you think? I say we try it out." Marcus made a move to put the blade to the little girl's face. Her daddy broke.

"Okay. Okay, man. Fuck!" he yelled. "Go in my closet. There's a false panel in there. I have, like, forty bands put up." Marcus displayed a sinister smile. He sat the child down and went to check out the spot.

After he located the money, he came back into the room, staring at Black N Mild, trying to decide whether to kill him or not. Ty told Marcus not to kill him, if he didn't have to. Her logic was, since she wasn't on the scene, Black N Mild wouldn't suspect her. Therefore, she could play him close, and hit him again.

Marcus stood there, gripping the knife repeatedly. His breathing became labored. He had an irresistible blood lust that needed to be sedated. Instead, he walked out of the room and out the front door. Much to Black N Mild's relief.


Two days later, Ty sat in the driver's seat of Pat's black-on-black 750Li, while Pat was laid up at the hotel. Ty took the car for a supposed breakfast run. She sat across the street from Carl's New Start Auto Parts, which was a cover up for a drug operation.

Through one of her tricks, she learned Carl, a 52-year-old mechanic, was also selling lots of cocaine out of his shop. She also learned he usually made deposits to the bank twice a week. After giving one of Carl's disgruntled workers some sloppy head, he confessed that Carl was due to make a drop that day.

Of course, Ty was out that same morning, supervising the play. She sat watching intently, as Carl hopped into his beat-up Grand Marquise, toting a black nylon bag. Ty checked her rearview. Marcus was parked in a black Chevy Cobalt, a few blocks back. "Showtime," she whispered to herself.

Carl cranked his car up and maneuvered out of the parking lot. Ty timed it, so she'd pull out right in front of him. From her Intel, she knew he only banked at Woodforest Bank on Uvalde. She also knew he always made a stop at a donut shop on Normandy, to grab a croissant. As well as a blueberry muffin. That's where they would strike.

The whole ride there, Ty drove in front, keeping a safe distance. Since she already knew his destination, she didn't have to worry about losing him.

Once they arrived at the donut shop, Ty hopped out the car first. Dressed in some red coochie cutter shorts with her ass cheeks hanging out and a yellow tank top. Nipples poking through the fabric. She made sure Carl got an eyeful.

Ty switched and swayed. Her booty cheeks jiggled as she walked into the store. She stood in front of the counter and waited. As soon as she saw Carl enter, she called Pat. "Heyy, baby. I'm at the shop right now. Yeah, they had an accident. So, what do you want?" Ty listened as Pat gave his order. Carl stared at her ass as he waited in line. "I think something's wrong with the car. I don't know if it's the alternator, or the battery but . . . I think we need to go get it checked."

Hearing this, Carl figured he had a great opening to begin a conversation. He waited until she ended her call, before he approached. "Um. Excuse me, Ms. Lady. I couldn't help but overhear you're having car trouble. I might be able to assist you. I'm a mechanic." Ty turned around and let him get a good look at her D cups. Her nipples poked out like two thimbles on her chest.

"Oh, okay. Well, I don't know what's wrong with it. It might be something wrong with the battery. Someone else said the alternator."

"Sometimes. When I'm sitting idly at the light, the car just shuts off," Ty claimed. As she wet her lips, Carl felt his cock twitch. He began to fantasize about her lips wrapped around his dick. He hadn't had a good shot of twat in almost a month. He was due for some, and didn't mind paying.

"Look, sweetie. Why don't you bring it to the shop

tomorrow? I'll take a look at it for you." Carl returned the look of seduction.

"Well. What are you about to do now? Maybe you can take a quick look, once you grab your food," Ty offered.

"Uhh. You know what? I can do that. Just give me a second to grab my stuff," Carl told her as he approached the counter. Few minutes later, they both grabbed their orders and headed out to the parking lot.

As soon as they exited the store, Carl dropped his food in shock. "What the fuck?" His passenger window has a softball sized hole in it. Courtesy of a window puncher. "No, no, no, no, no, no," he chanted as he ran over to assess the damage. He peered inside and could immediately tell, the nylon bag was gone. That meant so was the money. "Fuck!" He tilted his head back and screamed into the heavens.

"Is everything alright?" Ty timidly asked, from the safety of the sidewalk. Carl shook his head, looked at her and said, "I just got robbed."

"What? Are you serious? You want me to call the police?" Ty made a show of pulling out her phone and preparing to dial. Instinctively, Carl declined to let her call the police, but then he remembered, he's a legitimate business man. He ended up calling the police himself. Ty waited until the police came, so she could give a statement.

After parting ways with Carl, Ty called Marcus. He notified her that he made it out safely. "Imma take this nigga his car back," she told him. "I'll get him to drop me off at *our* room, so I can count it up." Ty hung up and headed back to the hotel room where Pat was unsuspectingly waiting for her. Another job well done.

Later that afternoon, Ty did her count. She realized she's almost at her goal. *$100,000!* She needed one more lick to get there. School was starting back in the next few days. She needed to take the kids shopping for school clothes. After spending $2,000 for everything they needed, Ty took them to the house she planned on buying.

It wasn't a mansion or anything, but for $80,000, it would be theirs to do as they wished. Later that night, after the kids went to bed, she crept over to Marcus's room. Ty was really starting to fall for the little nigga. He had that unwavering loyalty a woman is always in search of. He'd put his life on the line, time after time.

She'd stop cheating him with the breakdowns. He was now getting an equal share. She had been defaulting on her promise to Bo. Since that first day she put the $500 on his books when he was in the county, Ty hadn't deposited anything else. It's not that she didn't want to, she was just busy as hell. She really needed to go see him and let him know that she knew who the real killer was. But, if she did that, she'd have to explain how she knew.

Ty planned on hiring an appeal attorney for Bo. Then maybe she could tell the lawyer and the lawyer would tell him. Either way, she planned on telling Bo the truth before she died. Right now, she was living life with her young stud. She loved Bo, but was falling in love with her young goon.

She watched him grow into a cold-blooded killer, all for

her. Whenever she witnessed him work, it always got her coochie wet as the everglades. As they cuddled in bed, Ty felt it was time to tell Marcus the whole truth. She rubbed her fingers across his chest, as she called out his name. "Marcus. I need to tell you something, baby."

He immediately stopped what he was doing and gave her his undivided attention. "What is it, baby? What's on your mind?"

"Look. I don't know how to tell you this, so I'll just come right out and say it. I'm dying!"

Marcus leaned back. Eyebrows furrowed. "What you mean, you're dying?"

Ty began to cough. Her lungs caked with mucus. Her body shuddered as she struggled to continue on with her conversation. "Before I met you, I was diagnosed with Lupus, as well as Pancreatic cancer. The doctor told me, if I don't take my treatment, I'll have 6-8 months to live. Well, I wasn't about to fuck with that Chemo shit. I watched my paw paw go through with that. It tore my family apart. I'm not about to put my kids through the same thing. So, I said fuck it. That's why I've been going so hard. I'm trying to get a house, bought and paid for. That way, my kids will have at least somewhere to sleep when I'm gone."

The tears began to race down her face. She felt a great burden lifted. Being able to confide about her secret with the one she loved. Marcus looked at her with pure love, soaked in his eyes. "How much do you need to buy the house, baby?"

"Well. The house is $80,000. It's in 5th Ward."

"Marcus was befuddled. "Why would you wanna house in 5th Ward? Why not the Woodlands, or Conroe?

"Shit. I would love to get a house in the suburbs. But a bitch on a time limit. Gotta get what I can afford." Marcus sat quietly, contemplating something.

"Tomorrow, while the kids are in school. I want you to go house shopping. Hit up the Woodlands, or Humble at least. See what you can find." Ty looked into his eyes. She saw nothing but sincere love and affection. It's crazy. It took a man so young to finally give her what she'd been missing. She knew then, he'd do whatever needed to be done, to make sure her dream came true. For that, she loved him even more.

"Okay, baby," she whispered. She slid down the length of his body. Kissing him along the way. She trapped his heavy dick between her lips. For the first time since they'd met, Ty and Marcus made passionate love. All night long.


Mya had finally started back in school. Just a few months ago, she thought she was going to have to drop out in order to help take care of CJ. Her first day was spent catching up with all her old girlfriends from the neighborhood. The same ones she went to middle school and part of high school with.

The girls could be found in the cafeteria, checking out all the cute boys. One in particular caught Mya's eye. He was a Junior. Played Varsity football, and was cute as hell. 6 foot, brown skin, 190 lbs. Even though he was athletically built, his drip was like that of a D Boy's. Mya couldn't stop staring at him. Finally, he caught her looking. He smiled.

Mya blushed. She couldn't help it. Her heart began to

patter, her palms a sweaty mess. It wasn't as if she was some innocent little girl. She was already having sex like a grown woman. But it was something about the dude that made her body go haywire. "Mya! Mya! You listening?" Her homegirl—Kay Kay—kept snapping her fingers in Mya's face, trying to get her attention.

"Huh? What?"

"Girl. Where the hell did you go? I was asking, what class did you get for 1st period?"

Mya looked at her schedule. "Um. I got English with Mr. Mikleson." Their homegirl, Tiffany, scoffed.

"I heard he's gay."

"I don't care if he's gay or not. As long as he ain't racist, I'm cool." Mya reasoned. Her eyes kept drifting towards the football cutie. Kay Kay finally caught sight.

"Girl. Who you keep looking at?" Once Kay Kay saw who was in Mya's line of vision, she smiled. "Ohhh, okay. Yeah, girl, he's fine as fuck. That's Jeremiah. He's a Junior and starting cornerback for Varsity. He has a girlfriend, but you already know, that don't mean shit."

The rest of the crew began to laugh. In their eyes, only dudes that were off limits were the ones that belonged to them. Everyone else's men were up for grabs. "Kay Kay. How you know all that? We just started school," Mya questioned.

"Well. If you weren't MIA all summer, you'd have known. His Uncle Pat threw him a birthday bash over the summer. No Cap. That bitch was lit. They had it over July 4th weekend. That's where I got all the tea on him and his little cheerleader girlfriend, Roxy!"

Mya scrunched her face up. "Roxy?"

"Yeah? Short for Roxanne. She's Mexican and black," Kay Kay said with disdain. The first bell rang, signifying the students had five minutes to get to class. The crew dispersed, promising to meet back up at the same spot for lunch.

As Mya was taking her seat in English class, Jeremiah waltzed in with a 100 megawatt smile on his face. The air thickened. The nerves in her right leg wouldn't stop acting up. "Somebody sitting here?" Jeremiah asked, while pointing at the empty seat behind Mya.

She attempted to speak. Her voice caught in her throat. She settled for a simple shake of the head. "No."

"Bet. I'm Jeremiah. Everybody calls me J-Mah."

"Uhm. I'm Mya. Everybody calls me My, or Mya," she giggled nervously. Jeremiah sat down. Mr Mikleson entered the class minutes later.

Twenty minutes into the lesson, Jeremiah tapped her on the shoulder. She waited until the teacher was writing on the board before she turned to see what he wanted. "What?" She hissed.

"Here. Read this." He handed her a note.

*Wassup My. Look, I'm feeling your vibe. FrFr. I got a girl, but I'm trying to see if we can be special friends. If you feeling that, shoot me your number. I'll call you after foot-ball practice.*

Mya bit her bottom lip. Her first day of school and she snatched up something nice. She wrote her number down and slid the paper back to him. Jeremiah read it, and couldn't contain his smile. Mya was bad as hell. She was built like some of the chicks his uncle was messing with. He just knew. With a body like that, no way she was a virgin. His girl Roxy was cool, but Mya was on another level. He spent the rest of the class daydreaming about them having sex. Wondering what it would feel like.

## 16

MARCUS SAT BACK in his seat, brim low, watching Pat from the shadows. He'd been stalking him for a couple weeks now. Pat seemed to be one of those "hands on", do-everything- yourself type of guys. That would prove to be his undoing.

He watched as Pat picked up what he assumed to be money. This was his third trap house of the day. Sometimes he'd be with his right-hand man, KD, but most of the time, he was by himself.

Marcus studied the routes Pat took. He utilized the backstreets. No doubt, in order to avoid the cops on the main road. Now that Ty had confided in him about her illness and what her goals were, Marcus felt it was time to execute his plan.

Pat exited the trap, with yet another bag. Marcus pulled off and drove away. He utilized sort of the same tactic they used on Carl the mechanic. He already knew which route he was going to take, so he laid in wait.

Marcus found the perfect spot to spring the ambush. He parked, flipped the hazards and waited. It was a four-way stop, with big ditches on either side. Pat couldn't pass him up, unless he wanted to drive into a ditch.

Marcus reached into the backseat and grabbed the mini Draco. Seconds later, he checked his rearview. Sure enough, Pat was coming down the backstreet. Marcus had the element of surprise, but knew he had to act quick. Pat was a street nigga. Marcus couldn't give him time to analyze the situation. If he did, things could get messy.

As soon as Pat approached within 8 feet of Marcus's bumper, Marcus leapt out of the driver seat. Draco poised and ready. '*Bap! Bap! Bap! Bap! Bap!*' Marcus fucked the trigger, aiming for the head and chest. The windshield decimated, as he walked the older man down.

Pat hit the gas. The car lurched forward. Marcus jumped out the way, barely missing by inches. Pat's car veered into the ditch and crashed. Marcus crept up in the wreck, finger on the trigger.

Marcus squeezed. He had a full hundred-round clip and planned on using every last shell. The .762's chewed through glass and metal. Blood spatters could be seen decorating the seats, as Marcus approached the driver side door.

He peered inside. Pat laid on the floorboard; blood and glass littered his being. No breathing, no movement at all. He was dead.

Marcus began his search for the bag. He checked the front but didn't see it. Then, he checked the backseat. *Bingo!*

He opened the back door, snatched the bag and ran to his car. Heart pounding through his chest. He drove away, elated he was able to pull it off. He didn't know exactly how much he'd hit for. It really didn't matter; he planned on giving it all to Ty. That way, she could get a decent house for her and her kids.

Just thinking about Ty and her situation saddened him. He was madly in love with her, and God was trying to take her away. All he could do was make sure the time she did have left, they spent it together. Happy and fulfilled.

Now, he had to figure out if he should tell Ty about the Pat lick or not. She claimed what she and Pat had was just business, but Marcus didn't consult with her about taking Pat down. So, he decided he'd have to take this one to the grave.

After counting the contests of the bag, Marcus saw he'd hit for $86,472. It wasn't what he'd hoped for, but he was pretty sure if he added that with what they already had, Ty could buy a really nice house with it. He picked up his phone and texted her. She responded.

Ty: *kicking it wit Gino*

Gino was her newest business venture. He was a successful businessman, who was going to purchase the house, then transfer the deed in her name.

Marcus: *Did u find a house yet?*

Ty: *Matter fact, I did. Humble. $235,000. 4 bedroom 3 bath. Beautiful!*

Marcus: *Great. I gotta surprise for u. Hit me when you on your way.*

Ty: *Aight baby*

Marcus: *I love you*

Ty looked at the message for a second. Took a deep breath and then responded.

Ty: *I luv u 2 (heart emoji)*

She put the phone down and picked Gino's dick up. She exhaled deeply before opening up wide and stuffing him back into her mouth. She loved Marcus, but still had her goals to meet. Fucking Gino and sucking his dick was going to help her achieve those goals.

Gino wasn't what most women would call attractive. His hairline was receding. He acted as if he was scared to let it go. He was out of shape and—most devastatingly—he only had five inches of dick to work with.

But, with all that said, he was worth three million dollars. So, he had no trouble with the ladies. "Ssshit. That's it, baby. Suck this big ole dick," he urged her. Ty rolled her eyes at his misplaced self-assessment. She stuffed his entire cock in her mouth and still had some room to stick her tongue out and lap at his balls.

She pushed his legs back, exposing his crinkly asshole. Ty pulled back, allowing his dick to fall out her mouth. She dipped her head under his nuts, tracing the tip of her tongue around the rim of his shit hole. He shivered as if he was freezing cold. She hardened her tongue, pushing through his barrier and fucking him with the tip.

He moaned in delight. She jacked him off at a fevered pace. Sucking gently on his balls. "Oh, shit. Oh, shit. I'm 'bout to cum, girl. Fuck, I'm 'bout to cum."

Gino's dick jerked. Spurts of warm cock snot shot forth. Ty couldn't cover him up fast enough. The first shot splattered her face. The 2nd and 3rd filled her mouth, ballooning her cheeks. Ty closed her eyes, took one big gulp and swallowed everything he offered her.

Ty wanted to make sure, when Gino went home that night, he dreamt of her while his wife laid asleep next to him. Gino was the one that would clean her money up. Make her house a legit purchase. She just didn't want to hurt Marcus.

She could tell Marcus started feeling some type of way about her messing with other men. Even though it was for business purposes. Hopefully, Gino would be the last one.

Ty licked along his shaft, like a cat giving herself a bath. Once he was back fully erect, she strapped a Durex condom on and rode him until he came again. During the whole session, she hadn't come once. She didn't care, her mission was accomplished.

Antonio Tramain aka A-Train, just arrived back on Ferguson unit, via the Blue Bird. He'd left on bench warrant to resolve a pending case in a neighboring county. After twelve months and a guilty plea, he was back.

A-Train was 6'4", 260 lbs. A monster of a man. He'd been locked up for the past 16 years. Doing life for a murder. Dark-skinned, body covered in tattoos, Train looked the part of a deranged killer. A-Train was many things. One of them being, the estranged boyfriend of none other than Rose.

Train was known to be very jealous when it came to Rose. That jealousy would often lead to violence. If Rose would have known they were going to send Train back to

Ferguson, he would've never gotten involved with Bo. It was too late for all that now.

As soon as Train came through the back gates, he saw Double R. Double R was one of his patnas that dealt with punks also. Double R was excited to see his boy back on the ranch. "Train! Wassup, nigga? What they do for you?"

A-Train had been fighting a manslaughter charge out of Bryon County. He ended up singing 20 years, to be ran C.C. (Concurrent). "Shit. Them hoes gave me a dub. I ain't tripping. The L ate it up anyway. What's been going on around this bitch?"

"Aww, man. Your hoe out here wilding," Double R instigated.

Train's face hardened. "What you mean?"

"She fucking with some new nigga that just pulled up. They moved in together and everything."

"Say what? Man, I know that hoe ain't disrespecting like that. Say, bruh. *Whoever* that nigga is, tell him I'm trynna fuck with him on the yard. Soon as they call it!" A-Train was furious. He had a reputation on the unit, and Rose knew not to play with him. *That bitch got me fucked up. Imma snatch her ass up, when I see her,* he told himself.

Even though he'd been gone a year, he expected Rose to sit back and wait on him. "What block they stay on?" Train asked.

"Your old block. L block!"

"A'ight . . . well, look. I don't know what block they gonna put me on, but holla at Lieutenant Gains and see if he'll put me back over there. Until then, I'm on the yard every time they call it." Double couldn't help but smile. He was one of those messy ass niggas, who loved to see people getting into conflicts.

After Train went through Intake, he saw they'd put him on H Block. He immediately sent Rose a message, letting him know. *"Her man was back on the unit. And her ass better fall in line."* After he got settled in, he did a quick workout routine. He needed to get his blood flowing and his muscles tighten. Rec was in a few hours.

"Oh my God!" Rose exclaimed, as he read the kite Train had sent him. Bo was at the toilet reading a book called *Sex, Murder and God.* It was written by an author named Lo-Life.

"What's wrong?"

Rose began to tremble. It had been many nights, Train had put a foot in his ass, for what Train perceived as Rose *flirting.* He could just imagine what he would do about *this.*

"My x just pulled back up to the unit. It sounds like he's on some bullshit."

"What you mean? Y'all aren't together, so what's he tripping 'bout?"

Rose squeezed his eyes shut, before he spoke. "Well. Technically, we never broke up. He went on bench warrant and had been gone a year. Naturally, I didn't think he was coming back."

Bo could tell, Rose was visibly shaken. "So what, you trynna fuck with him?"

"Hell naw. That nigga's always trynna beat a bitch's ass. No, ma'am!" Rose proclaimed.

"Look out, Bo," an inmate by the name of Lil 5th called out, as he approached Bo and Rose's cell.

"Wassup?" Bo answered back.

"Say, Double R told me to pull up on you. Go to rec tonight. That nigga A-Trains's trynna fuck with you." Lil 5th glanced at Rose when he said it, silently accusing him of once again starting some bullshit.

Bo wasn't afraid one bit. One thing he knew how to do very well is: punch a nigga down. He'd been fighting his whole life. "Tell that nigga, that's a bet." With that, it was understood. Bo told Rose to hit the day room, while he loosened up. He didn't want to underestimate anybody. Even Ali got beat.

Later that evening, rec was called. It seemed as if the whole unit was in the yard. Everyone was segregated into groups. Being that Bo was solo, he was on his own. Still, they had niggas from his city that respected a real nigga, so they told him they wouldn't let him get jumped. Others felt they didn't want to get involved with no homosexual beef. *So be it.*

Train was a Blood from Austin. Due to the fact "the pound" frowned upon homosexual activity, he wasn't supposed to be reppin. But because of his reputation and get down, he pretty much did what he wanted. As soon as the guards counted, the two met behind the handball court.

Rose, along with a group of punks, stood on the side-lines watching. Waiting on the verdict. Rose hoped and prayed Bo showed that work. If not, Train was going to put a foot in Rose's ass.

Train sized Bo up. Bo was shorter and weighed less. Train honestly felt as if Bo looked soft. "Say, nigga, I'ma give you a chance to gone bow down. Get out the way, and send my hoe back. I know I was gone. You ain't know no better. So, I'm willing to give you a pass."

Bo looked at him and smirked. "Nigga, I ain't come down here to do no bumping. If we gone punch, then *ding ding*."

Both men advanced and threw their guards up. Each hesitant to throw the first punch. Train finally committed and threw a fast right straight. Bo slipped under the jab, but didn't counter. He wanted a little bit more Intel, before he went on the offensive.

Train threw another straight. This time, when Bo went to slip, Train threw a short left hook that grazed Bo on his chin. That's what Bo was waiting on. He needed to see if Train actually had any strategy. Could he think? Or, was he just a nigga that used his size?

Bo backed up, forcing Train to pursue. Bo waited until Train advanced, before throwing a feint jab. Train flinched, Bo dipped, and came up with a right cross. It landed flush on Train's chin. Train stumbled, but quickly shook it off. They squared back up.

Train shuffled right, dipped once, dipped again, then came up releasing a vicious hard left hook. Bo put his left guard up, taking the brunt of the blow. But the punch had so much power behind it, it went through Bo's guard and still connected soundly against Bo's temple. Bo's skull shook, but he maintained.

When Train tried to follow up with a knockout right hook, Bo dipped low and came up with a dangerous upper-cut. Train's head snapped back. He stumbled. Bo smelled blood.

Seeing Train dazed, Bo dipped and stepped into a tremendous right hook. A loud crack reverberated across the rec yard. Train's body went limp. He fell face first into the dirt and grass. *Sleep!*

At first, no one said a word. Everyone seemed stunned that A-Train was fast asleep. He'd been terrorizing the unit for years. Many people didn't like Train, but were too scared to challenge him. To see him laid low was shocking. Then, like a small ripple in a pond, the snickers came. Followed by the giggles. Then, the full out laughter. Suddenly, the chants and taunts began. "He slept that nigga," and "that's what his bitch ass gets".

Bo wasn't the type of dude to brag or boast. Plus, knocking opponents out was something he did on the regular. Instead, he quietly left Train on the ground and made his way back over to the weight set. Before long, Rose made his way over to him, grinning like a Cheshire cat. "What you smiling 'bout?" Bo asked while setting the weights up on the bench press machine.

"You did that," Rose complimented. The look on his face read, pure infatuation. Bo smirked, then thought about something.

"Rose. I don't need to be hearing 'bout you all in that nigga's face. You hear me?" Rose dropped the playful demeanor. He knew Bo was being serious as a heart attack.

"Yes, Daddy, I hear you. I don't have no reason to be in any niggas face but yours." Satisfied with his response, Bo got underneath the weight bench to begin his workout. Rose just sat there, admiring his knight in shining armor.

Ten minutes after he was knocked out, Train was finally able to wake up and shake the cobwebs off. He stood across the rec yard, mugging Bo. Pure hatred blazed in his eyes. "You a'ight, Train?" Double R asked as he approached the fallen giant.

"Yeah, I'm good, my nigga. Bitch ass nigga just got a lucky punch in," Train claimed. "It's all good though. I got something for his bitch ass." Little did Bo know, this was the beginning of a feud that would cost him more than he bargained for.


Ty couldn't believe it. Her dream had finally been realized. Marcus, her two kids and her, stood in the living room of her brand new home. She went ahead and found and bought a home in Humble. A neighborhood called Kenswick off 1960.

The house was a two-story, four-bedroom brick home, with a huge backyard. They wanted $225k, but Gino knew the seller and talked them down to $195k. With the money she'd saved up, Ty still needed help. Marcus already had intentions on helping. With what he peeled Pat for, they had more than enough to purchase the home.

After the sale was finalized, Gino transferred the deed over to Mya and CJ. Marcus made sure the house was fully furnished. Nothing too extravagant. The luxuries could come later.

Even though they'd decided to give their relationship a chance, Marcus and Ty agreed to sleep in separate rooms. They didn't want to confuse the kids. They viewed Marcus as the "fun" uncle, who loved to take them to Funplex, and out to eat for ice cream and slushies.

Ty knew, if the kids saw them shacking up, they'd assume that Ty gave up on their daddy. That definitely wasn't the case. She was just lonely and in desperate need of some companionship. "Momma, momma. Why does Mya get the big bedroom?" Little CJ whined from the top of the stairs.

"Because I'm older, stupid."

"Mya. Don't call your brother stupid," Ty chastised her. Ty looked at CJ. With a patient smile, she explained. "She gets the bigger room because she's older, baby. When she gets big like mommy and moves out, then you'll have her room. Okay?"

CJ nodded and ran back into his room. Mya was already on the phone, bragging about the new house. Ty promised they could finish out the school year at their old school. So, that meant a commute every morning back to the Eastside. She didn't mind. As long as her kids were happy and healthy, she was good.

Now that the house was purchased, she needed a source of income to sustain the bills. She told herself she'd stop robbing and try to find a legitimate job. Until then, she'd have to figure out something.

She knew Marcus still had some money. She didn't want to lean on him too much. Ty didn't want her kids to be at his mercy when she died. Just then, she thought about Bo and wondered what he was doing at that very moment. Would he be proud of the moves she was making? Now that she'd accomplished her main goal, she needed to take the kids to go see their daddy. She'd told Bo she was going to pull up, but never seemed to find the time. It seemed like she always had something to do.

"What's on your mind, baby?" Marcus asked, sensing her contemplation. Ty looked at him with a small smile.

"Nothing, babe. I'm just glad my kids and I have you in our lives. You're truly a blessing. Can you make me a promise?"

"Sure. What is it?"

Ty's voice began to crack under the emotional strain. "Can you . . . Can you please continue to look after my kids for me? You know, their daddy is gone and they don't have anyone else." Ty opened up completely.

Marcus grabbed her hand with his right and tilted her chin up with his left. "I got you, baby. I promise. I'll look after them with my life." Ty felt his words deep in her core. She knew he meant them with every fiber in him. The sacrifices the young nigga had made for her and her kids caused her to fall in love with him.

She still loved Bo, but the chances of her being in Bo's arms before she died was slim to none. Ty wanted to spend her last days on earth happy. It seemed Marcus could provide that. He leaned in and gave her a sensual kiss.

Ty moaned as she melted into his body. Lost in the moment of pure, unfiltered passion. Marcus reached down and cuffed her ass cheeks. She caressed the front of his jeans, gripping his dick through the fabric. She wanted to taste him. Needed to feel him deep inside.

Her desires took hold of her. So focused on her primal need, she forgot her two children were upstairs. She reached into his jeans and pulled out his heavy dick. Her heartbeat quickened. Marcus gazed at her in anticipation. Ty began to drop to her knees when . . . "Momma! Momma!"

CJ appeared at the top of the stairs. Ty and Marcus hurriedly broke apart. Marcus rushed into the kitchen to fix himself. Ty, clearly flustered, looked up at her son. "What's wrong, Jr.?"

"Do you think we can take a picture of my room and send it to dad?"

Her heart felt a slight pang. "Uhh, sure. I'll get my phone and we can take some pictures." Ty went to the kitchen to retrieve her phone out of her purse. Marcus stood there. An embarrassed look on his face.

Ty felt bad. She couldn't give him complete dominance of her heart. She walked up to him and whispered, "I'm sorry." Then kissed him, before heading upstairs to take pictures for her baby daddy.

## 17

"OKAY, girl. So, what you gone tell your momma?" Kay Kay asked.

"Shit. I'll tell her we gone be at your house. You know she trusts your momma the most," Mya replied. Both girls were plotting on what to do after school the next day. Since they stayed across town, Ty was allowing Mya to go to her friend Kay Kay's house after school. Picking her up, around 6-7 p.m. That would give the girls a few hours to spend some time together.

What Ty didn't know was that Mya had no intentions on going to Kay Kay's house. In fact, Mya intended skipping the last period to go kick it with Jeremiah. "A'ight, well, my momma gotta work an extra shift. So, that's perfect. Imma have my lil boo thang, Anthony, come through. When you and Jeremiah get done, call me and let me know you're on your way." Once they had their plans set and perfected, they hung up and prepared for school the next day.

School was an utter torture for Mya. She kept looking up at the clock every five minutes. It seemed time was going backwards. She desperately wanted to lock Jeremiah in, and was worried something was going to happen and mess all that up.

Her right leg wouldn't stop bouncing. She couldn't stop chewing her bottom lip. Her eyes darted back to the clock for the hundredth time. She had four minutes until quitting time.

Jeremiah already texted her, letting her know he would be waiting in the student parking lot. All the other students in her class had their textbooks out and opened. Hers was closed and in her backpack. 'Riiinnnnggggg' *Finally!*

Mya shot out of her seat like a heat seeking missile, the teacher yelling reminders for the work assignment they had over the weekend. She made it to the parking lot in record time. Sure enough, Jeremiah was waiting for her, sitting in his brand new triple black Dodge Durango Pat bought him for his birthday.

He saw her, his eyes sparkled. He wet his lips. Even though she was just as thirsty as he appeared to be, Mya played it cool. "I'm really surprised you're here. I thought you was gone be all cap," she told him.

Jeremiah slunk back in insult. "Me. Cap? I don't do no capping, momma. Everything big facts with me," he boasted. Mya jumped into the passenger seat. His eyes drunk her in. Her shapely legs. Her melon sized titties. *She's definitely stacked,* he thought. Jeremiah felt extremely nervous. For some reason, he didn't feel his sex game was going to be adequate enough. He never had any complaints, but then again, he'd never messed with a chick like Mya.

Mya flipped the visor down, and acted as if she didn't notice him jocking her drip. He push-started the whip and brought the engine to life. "Where we going?" Mya asked. She honestly didn't care about the destination, just the events once they got there.

"One of my uncle's duck off spots. He just got out the hospital, so he's laid up at the crib with my Aunt J. We don't have to worry 'bout him popping up on us," Jeremiah informed her.

"So what? He just gave you your own set of keys?"

"Well. Not really. He kind of let me use the spot once and I made copies of the keys," Jeremiah said with a conspiratorial smile.

"Boy, you bad." Mya smirked, while shaking her head. On the outside she appeared cool and calm. Inside, she was a nervous wreck. She knew what he wanted. The same thing all boys his age wanted. She just hoped he liked what she had to offer. She wasn't a virgin, but she also knew he'd had his fair share. Her experience might not be up to par. The last thing she wanted, for him to view her sex game as lame.

They pulled up to a set of apartments on the Beltway named Alta Crossing. Mya had to admit, they were nice. Way better than the apartments her family used to stay in. When she walked in, she felt at ease. The decor was stylish and trending. The carpet was plush. The appliances were stainless steel. The countertops were granite. If this was his uncle's duck off, she would love to see where he called home.

Mya made an attempt to sit down in the living room. Jeremiah had other plans. "Naw, naw. Follow me." Mya did what he asked and allowed him to lead her into the master bedroom. The bed was king-size. Red satin sheets and a red and black velvet lined comforter laid on top. Even the pillows had satin pillow cases. A black leather loveseat sat pressed against the wall. On the adjacent wall hung a 64" Samsung flat screen. Mya didn't want to seem too presumptuous, so she sat on the sofa. "You smoke?" Jeremiah asked while pulling out one of the dresser drawers.

Mya didn't smoke, but didn't want to seem weird. So she lied. "Yeah, I smoke. What you got?"

"Shit. Really, I don't know. He only smokes the best though." Jeremiah pulled out a sack and some cigarillos. After breaking the buds down and twisting them up, they were both high as giraffe pussy. Mya's whole body tingled. She felt so relaxed. Before she realized it, Jeremiah was all over her, grabbing at her titties and rubbing on her pussy. She reached for his piece, but Jeremiah refused her. "Naw, baby. Let me go first," he whispered. Mya sat back, and enjoyed the sensation he was giving her. She just prayed he enjoyed it, when it was her turn.


Meme was frustrated as hell. She hadn't heard anything from Pat in a couple weeks. She tried to call his phone. His wife answered, so she hung up. Meme didn't know if she'd done something to upset him or not. Deep down inside, she felt something else was going on. She just couldn't put her finger on it.

Not knowing what else to do, she hopped on the

beltway and headed to the same apartment Pat used to always take her to. Meme didn't know what to expect. She hoped she'd bump into somebody that could tell her Pat's whereabouts.

She exited the freeway and turned into the complex. So many memories came flooding in. She remembered how he used to fuck her on the back patio, in the middle of the night. How she used to suck his dick, while he talked to his wife. Meme, swallowing his cum with delight. She even remembered the threesome she gave him after a wild night at the strip club.

Now, she hadn't heard a peep from him. *Nothing!* It's like he dropped off the face of the earth. Meme sat in the car, just waiting and watching. For what? She had no idea. After an hour and a half, she finally decided it was time to leave.

As she cranked the car up, the door to the apartment swung open. She couldn't believe her eyes. Mya was walking out of the apartment. *Can't be!* She thought. *Is Pat fucking on my lil niece? Please don't tell me that nigga done stooped that low,* Meme questioned herself.

Then, she saw Pat's nephew and it all made sense. If someone knew where Pat was, it would be his favorite nephew. Meme hopped out and approached the couple. When Mya saw Meme, her heart dropped. She stutter-stepped and almost turned around.

The last thing she needed was Meme telling her mom she saw her coming out of an apartment with some boy, while she was supposed to be at school. "Heyy, Mya. What's been up?" Meme sang out.

"Hey, Aunt Meme. Nothing much. Just over visiting a

friend," Mya hurriedly explained. Meme made a show of glancing at her watch to let Mya know *she* knew Mya was skipping school.

"Ain't you Jeremiah, Pat's nephew? You remember me?" Meme asked.

"Yeah, that's me. And of course, I remember you," Jeremiah told her. The last time he'd seen Meme, he was spending the night with his uncle at the same duck off spot they were at. He walked in the living room and found Meme with a mouth full of his uncle's dick. Jeremiah stood there for minutes, watching Meme gobble up dick like a porn star. They even caught him watching. Neither Pat nor Meme stopped what they were doing.

Once, while Pat's hand was behind Meme's head, pushing her further and further down into his lap, he gave Jeremiah the silent invite. Basically, asking if he would like to come sample some of Meme's goods.

Jeremiah was a little more timid then. He was having sex, but he hadn't opened up yet. He told himself, if he ever got the chance again, he'd stand up in the pussy. By the look that passed between the both of them, Meme knew exactly what he was thinking. "Y'all know each other?" Mya asked suspiciously. Obviously picking up on the vibes.

"Oh, yeah, girl. I mess with his uncle Pat. Matter of fact, I lost my phone and didn't have his number memorized. That's why I came out here. To see if I could catch up to him," Meme lied.

"Unc's at the crib. He just got released from the hospital. Someone ran him off the road and he crashed into a ditch. That was like 3-4 weeks ago. He was in really bad shape, but he's better now."

The relief on Meme's face was evident. The whole time, she assumed Pat was ducking and dodging her. When in fact, he had been badly injured. "Ohhh, okay. That explains it. Usually he would have been got in touch with me. He knows where I stay, but um . . . I'll let you kids get back to doing y'all." Before she turned to leave, she added. "Oh. Mya, I had gone by that place y'all was at the last time I saw y'all. I notice y'all aren't living there anymore."

Meme didn't want to throw shade on Mya for having to live in a motel. "Uhh, yeah. We moved, Aunt Meme. We stay in Humble now. Momma bought us a two-story house out there."

The look of shock was evident on Meme's face. She couldn't believe Ty bought a house. She was just homeless a couple months ago. "Oh, she must have gotten approved for HUD or something," Meme asked suggestively.

"Naw. Momma bought it in cash," Mya corrected her. *Impossible.* Meme needed to see it for herself.

"Girrll. I need to come see this." Mya went ahead and gave Meme the new address. Then, Meme pulled her out of earshot from Jeremiah. "Don't worry. I won't tell your momma," she assured Mya.

A great weight lifted from Mya's shoulders as relief set in. She felt if her mom found out she skipped school, she'd make her transfer and go to Humble High School. When Mya and CJ were staying with Meme, she was the one putting Mya on game. There were some things Meme knew that Ty never found out. Mya felt she could trust her with her secret.

After they went their separate ways, Meme punched the address in her GPS, and made her way to Humble.

. . .

When she pulled up to the house, she couldn't believe what her eyes were seeing. Immediately, jealousy reared its ugly head. The house was beautiful. The lawn was well manicured. The neighborhood seemed quiet and peaceful.

Meme couldn't understand how Ty could afford to buy a house, cash! Something wasn't adding up. She hopped out and rang the bell.

Minutes later, a sexy but obviously young man answered the door. A pair of grey joggers and a beater, his muscles were bulging. Meme couldn't help but sneak a peek at his dick print. "Can I help you?" Marcus asked.

"I'm looking for Shatyra. Is she home?"

"Oh no. She's not here right now."

"Aunt Meme!" Little CJ screamed with joy. His little self couldn't contain his excitement. He ran to the door to greet her.

"Heyy, Pooh Bear. What's been up?" She grabbed him into a hug.

"Nothing. We moved."

"I see that. Where's your momma at?"

"She left. She'll be back in a little bit," he informed her. Seeing the familiarity between the two, Marcus offered Meme to come in. Once inside she could tell the house was scarcely furnished.

"Oh. I'm Meme by the way. Ty and I have been best friends for most of our lives. We're practically sisters," she claimed. Neglecting to mention that her and Ty hadn't talked in months.

"I'm Marcus. I'm just a friend of the family." *A friend of the family, my ass!* In Meme's mind, Ty had a little boy toy she was shacking up with. Meme checked him over once more and felt she may need to get a sample of what he had in the joggers, one of these days.

CJ offered to give her the tour. She reluctantly allowed him to lead the way. What Meme wanted was to learn more about the mysterious Marcus. What was his role in Ty acquiring the new house?

After about forty-five minutes, Meme decided it was time to go. Plus, Ty hadn't come back and she wasn't quite sure of what her reaction would be. Meme figured, she'd try and catch up to Ty on another day. Maybe on neutral ground. One on one!

"*Ainty*, can you take a picture? So, I can send it to my daddy," CJ asked. Meme had totally forgotten about Bo. It seemed like everybody did. Well, except his only son. Meme wondered what Bo had been up to. She'd heard he was messing with homosexuals now. If he was to win his appeal, she definitely wasn't letting him get up in her goodies any longer.

"Sure thing, Pooh Bear. She sat with him on the couch and proceeded to take selfies. She noticed Marcus was in a couple of the frames. He was talking idly on his cell phone in the kitchen. She didn't know why, but something told her she needed to make sure he was in the picture also.

After taking three different shots, she told CJ she would get them developed and bring them back, so he could send them to his daddy.

Two weeks later, CJ was playing on his miniature basketball goal in the front yard. Ty was in the kitchen cooking. Marcus left to go to the grocery store, and Mya was at her *friends'* house, yet again.

A black sedan turned on their street and crept to a stop, twenty feet away from their front door. Parked in front of a blue and white house. For ten minutes, no one emerged from the vehicle. It just sat there, idly waiting. *Watching.*

CJ missed a rebound. The ball ricocheted off the curb and rolled down the street. Stopping, three feet away from the black sedan. Just as CJ walked up to grab the ball, the front passenger door opened up. He jumped, startled. Then, recognition sat in. After a small conversation, CJ hopped inside the car, and was never seen or heard from, again.


Thirty minutes after CJ left, Marcus turned down their street. He noticed CJ's basketball; it had traveled halfway down the road. He stopped the car, scooped it up and continued on to the house. Once he walked in with the groceries, he called out to CJ. No answer. *Maybe he went upstairs.*

He found Ty cooking chicken in the kitchen. "Here goes the rest of what you needed," he told her as he gave her a kiss on the cheek.

"Baby. Can you tell CJ to come in, so he can get ready for dinner?"

Marcus looked at Ty confused. "What do you mean? He's already inside the house."

"Huh? Baby, I would know if he came into the house." Realization hit. She ran outside yelling his name. "CJ! . . . CJ! Baby, where are you?" They searched everywhere. Even places they knew he would never go. Just as they both came to the conclusion, something horrible had occurred, Ty received a call from a private number. "Hello?"

*"We have your son. We want two hundred and fifty thousand dollars by the end of the week, or he's dead. If you go to the cops, then he's dead. This is sudden death. Clock's ticking."* The caller hung up. Ty's whole body crumbled. She collapsed on the floor, crying for her baby boy and asking God why her, why always her?

To Be Continued . . .

# LOCK DOWN PUBLICATIONS AND CA$H PRESENTS

## ASSISTED PUBLISHING PACKAGES

| BASIC PACKAGE | UPGRADED PACKAGE |
|---|---|
| $499 | $800 |
| Editing | Typing |
| Cover Design | Editing |
| Formatting | Cover Design |
| | Formatting |

| ADVANCE PACKAGE | LDP SUPREME PACKAGE |
|---|---|
| $1,200 | $1,500 |
| Typing | Typing |
| Editing | Editing |
| Cover Design | Cover Design |
| Formatting | Formatting |
| Copyright registration | Copyright registration |
| Proofreading | Proofreading |
| Upload book to Amazon | Set up Amazon account |
| | Upload book to Amazon |
| | Advertise on LDP, Amazon and Facebook Page |

Submission Guidelines

Submit the first three chapters of your completed manuscript to ldpsubmissions@gmail.com. In the subject line add Your Book's Title. The manuscript must be in a Word Doc file and sent as an attachment. Document should be in Times New Roman, double spaced, and in size 12 font. Also, provide your synopsis and full contact information. If sending multiple submissions, they must each be in a separate email.

Have a story but no way to send it electronically? You can still submit to LDP/Ca$h Presents. Send in the first three chapters, written or typed, of your completed manuscript to:

LDP: Submissions Dept
P.O. Box 944
Stockbridge, GA 30281-9998

*DO NOT send original manuscript. Must be a duplicate.*
Provide your synopsis and a cover letter containing your full contact information.

Thanks for considering LDP and Ca$h Presents.

# NEW RELEASES

BLOODLINE OF A SAVAGE 1&2
THESE VICIOUS STREETS 1&2
RELENTLESS GOON
RELENTLESS GOON 2
BY PRINCE A. TAUHID

THE BUTTERFLY MAFIA 1-3
BY FUMIYA PAYNE

A THUG'S STREET PRINCESS 1&2
BY MEESHA

CITY OF SMOKE 2
BY MOLOTTI

STEPPERS 1,2&3
THE REAL BADDIES OF CHI-RAQ
BY KING RIO

THE LANE 1&2
BY KEN-KEN SPENCE

THUG OF SPADES 1&2
LOVE IN THE TRENCHES 2
CORNER BOYS
BY COREY ROBINSON

TIL DEATH 3

BY ARYANNA

THE BIRTH OF A GANGSTER 4
BY DELMONT PLAYER

PRODUCT OF THE STREETS 1&2
BY DEMOND "MONEY" ANDERSON

NO TIME FOR ERROR
BY KEESE

MONEY HUNGRY DEMONS
BY TRANAY ADAMS

STANDING ON HER BUSINESS 2
BY DG SANTANA

TENDER
BY KHUFU

HUB CITY MENACE
BY JAQUILLE M. WHITE

COUNTDOWN TO A KILLA
*CLOCK'S TICKING*
BY LO-LIFE

Coming Soon from Lock Down Publications/Ca$h Presents

IF YOU CROSS ME ONCE 6
ANGEL V
By Anthony Fields

IMMA DIE BOUT MINE 5
By Aryanna

A THUGS STREET PRINCESS 3
By Meesha

PRODUCT OF THE STREETS 3
By Demond Money Anderson

CORNER BOYS 2
By Corey Robinson

THE MURDER QUEENS 6&7
By Michael Gallon

CITY OF SMOKE 3
By Molotti

CONFESSIONS OF A DOPE BOY
By Nicholas Lock

THA TAKEOVER
By Keith Chandler

BETRAYAL OF A G 2
By Ray Vinci

CRIME BOSS
By Playa Ray

Available Now

RESTRAINING ORDER 1 & 2
By CA$H & Coffee

LOVE KNOWS NO BOUNDARIES 1-3
By Coffee

RAISED AS A GOON I, II, III & IV
BRED BY THE SLUMS I, II, III
BLAST FOR ME I & II
ROTTEN TO THE CORE I II III
A BRONX TALE I, II, III
DUFFLE BAG CARTEL I II III IV V VI
HEARTLESS GOON I II III IV V
A SAVAGE DOPEBOY I II
DRUG LORDS I II III
CUTTHROAT MAFIA I II
KING OF THE TRENCHES
By Ghost

LAY IT DOWN I & II
LAST OF A DYING BREED I II
BLOOD STAINS OF A SHOTTA I & II III
By Jamaica

LOYAL TO THE GAME I II III
LIFE OF SIN I, II III
By TJ & Jelissa

IF LOVING HIM IS WRONG…I & II
LOVE ME EVEN WHEN IT HURTS I II III
By Jelissa

PUSH IT TO THE LIMIT
By Bre' Hayes

BLOODY COMMAS I & II
SKI MASK CARTEL I, II & III
KING OF NEW YORK I II, III IV V
RISE TO POWER I II III
COKE KINGS I II III IV V
BORN HEARTLESS I II III IV
KING OF THE TRAP I II
By T.J. Edwards

WHEN THE STREETS CLAP BACK I & II III
THE HEART OF A SAVAGE I II III IV
MONEY MAFIA I II
LOYAL TO THE SOIL I II III
By Jibril Williams

A DISTINGUISHED THUG STOLE MY HEART I
II & III
LOVE SHOULDN'T HURT I II III IV
RENEGADE BOYS 1-4
PAID IN KARMA 1-3

SAVAGE STORMS 1-3
AN UNFORESEEN LOVE 1-3
BABY, I'M WINTERTIME COLD 1-3
A THUG'S STREET PRINCESS 1&2
By Meesha

A GANGSTER'S CODE 1-3
A GANGSTER'S SYN 1-3
THE SAVAGE LIFE 1-3
CHAINED TO THE STREETS 1-3
BLOOD ON THE MONEY 1-3
A GANGSTA'S PAIN 1-3
BEAUTIFUL LIES AND UGLY TRUTHS
CHURCH IN THESE STREETS
By J-Blunt

CUM FOR ME 1-8
An LDP Erotica Collaboration

BLOOD OF A BOSS 1-5
SHADOWS OF THE GAME
TRAP BASTARD
By Askari

THE STREETS BLEED MURDER 1-3
THE HEART OF A GANGSTA 1-3
By Jerry Jackson

WHEN A GOOD GIRL GOES BAD
By Adrienne

THE COST OF LOYALTY 1-3
By Kweli

BRIDE OF A HUSTLA 1-3
THE FETTI GIRLS 1-3
CORRUPTED BY A GANGSTA 1-4
BLINDED BY HIS LOVE
THE PRICE YOU PAY FOR LOVE 1-3
DOPE GIRL MAGIC 1-3
By Destiny Skai

A KINGPIN'S AMBITION
A KINGPIN'S AMBITION II
I MURDER FOR THE DOUGH
By Ambitious

TRUE SAVAGE 1-7
DOPE BOY MAGIC 1-3
MIDNIGHT CARTEL 1-3
CITY OF KINGZ 1&2
NIGHTMARE ON SILENT AVE
THE PLUG OF LIL MEXICO 1&2
CLASSIC CITY
By Chris Green

A GANGSTER'S REVENGE 1-4
THE BOSS MAN'S DAUGHTERS 1-5
A SAVAGE LOVE 1&2
BAE BELONGS TO ME 1&2
A HUSTLER'S DECEIT 1-3
WHAT BAD BITCHES DO 1-3

SOUL OF A MONSTER 1-3
KILL ZONE
A DOPE BOY'S QUEEN 1-3
TIL DEATH 1-3
IMMA DIE BOUT MINE 1-4
By Aryanna

A DOPEBOY'S PRAYER
By Eddie "Wolf" Lee

THE KING CARTEL 1-3
By Frank Gresham

THESE NIGGAS AIN'T LOYAL 1-3
By Nikki Tee

GANGSTA SHYT 1-3
By CATO

THE ULTIMATE BETRAYAL
By Phoenix

BOSS'N UP 1-3
By Royal Nicole

I LOVE YOU TO DEATH
By Destiny J

I RIDE FOR MY HITTA
I STILL RIDE FOR MY HITTA
By Misty Holt

LOVE & CHASIN' PAPER
By Qay Crockett

TO DIE IN VAIN
SINS OF A HUSTLA
By ASAD

BROOKLYN HUSTLAZ
By Boogsy Morina

BROOKLYN ON LOCK 1 & 2
By Sonovia

GANGSTA CITY
By Teddy Duke

A DRUG KING AND HIS DIAMOND 1-3
A DOPEMAN'S RICHES
HER MAN, MINE'S TOO 1&2
CASH MONEY HO'S
THE WIFEY I USED TO BE 1&2
PRETTY GIRLS DO NASTY THINGS
By Nicole Goosby

LIPSTICK KILLAH 1-3
CRIME OF PASSION 1-3
FRIEND OR FOE 1-3
By Mimi

TRAPHOUSE KING 1-3
KINGPIN KILLAZ 1-3

STREET KINGS 1&2
PAID IN BLOOD 1&2
CARTEL KILLAZ 1-3
DOPE GODS 1&2
By Hood Rich

THE STREETS ARE CALLING
By Duquie Wilson

STEADY MOBBN' 1-3
THE STREETS STAINED MY SOUL 1-3
By Marcellus Allen

WHO SHOT YA 1-3
SON OF A DOPE FIEND 1-4
HEAVEN GOT A GHETTO 1&2
SKI MASK MONEY 1&2
By Renta

GORILLAZ IN THE BAY 1-4
TEARS OF A GANGSTA 1/&2
3X KRAZY 1&2
STRAIGHT BEAST MODE 1&2
By DE'KARI

TRIGGADALE 1-3
MURDA WAS THE CASE 1-3
By Elijah R. Freeman

SLAUGHTER GANG 1-3
RUTHLESS HEART 1-3

By Willie Slaughter

GOD BLESS THE TRAPPERS 1-3
THESE SCANDALOUS STREETS 1-3
FEAR MY GANGSTA 1-5
THESE STREETS DON'T LOVE NOBODY 1-2
BURY ME A G 1-5
A GANGSTA'S EMPIRE 1-4
THE DOPEMAN'S BODYGAURD 1&2
THE REALEST KILLAZ 1-3
THE LAST OF THE OGS 1-3
By Tranay Adams

MARRIED TO A BOSS 1-3
By Destiny Skai & Chris Green

KINGZ OF THE GAME 1-7
CRIME BOSS 1-3
By Playa Ray

FUK SHYT
By Blakk Diamond

DON'T F#CK WITH MY HEART 1&2
By Linnea

ADDICTED TO THE DRAMA 1-3
IN THE ARM OF HIS BOSS
By Jamila

LOYALTY AIN'T PROMISED 1&2

By Keith Williams

YAYO 1-4
A SHOOTER'S AMBITION 1&2
BRED IN THE GAME
By S. Allen

TRAP GOD 1-3
RICH $AVAGE 1-3
MONEY IN THE GRAVE 1-3
CARTEL MONEY
By Martell Troublesome Bolden

FOREVER GANGSTA 1&2
GLOCKS ON SATIN SHEETS 1&2
By Adrian Dulan

TOE TAGZ 1-4
LEVELS TO THIS SHYT 1&2
IT'S JUST ME AND YOU
By Ah'Million

KINGPIN DREAMS 1-3
RAN OFF ON DA PLUG
By Paper Boi Rari

THE STREETS MADE ME 1-3
By Larry D. Wright

CONFESSIONS OF A GANGSTA 1-4
CONFESSIONS OF A JACKBOY 1-3

CONFESSIONS OF A HITMAN
By Nicholas Lock

I'M NOTHING WITHOUT HIS LOVE
SINS OF A THUG
TO THE THUG I LOVED BEFORE
A GANGSTA SAVED XMAS
IN A HUSTLER I TRUST
By Monet Dragun

QUIET MONEY 1-3
THUG LIFE 1-3
EXTENDED CLIP 1&2
A GANGSTA'S PARADISE
By Trai'Quan

CAUGHT UP IN THE LIFE 1-3
THE STREETS NEVER LET GO 1-3
By Robert Baptiste

NEW TO THE GAME 1-3
MONEY, MURDER & MEMORIES 1-3
By Malik D. Rice

CREAM 2-3
THE STREETS WILL TALK
By Yolanda Moore

THE STREETS WILL NEVER CLOSE 1-3
By K'ajji

LIFE OF A SAVAGE 1-4
A GANGSTA'S QUR'AN 1-4
MURDA SEASON 1-3
GANGLAND CARTEL 1-3
CHI'RAQ GANGSTAS 1-4
KILLERS ON ELM STREET 1-3
JACK BOYZ N DA BRONX 1-3
A DOPEBOY'S DREAM 1-3
JACK BOYS VS DOPE BOYS 1-3
COKE GIRLZ
COKE BOYS
SOSA GANG 1&2
BRONX SAVAGES
BODYMORE KINGPINS
BLOOD OF A GOON
By Romell Tukes

CONCRETE KILLA 1-3
VICIOUS LOYALTY 1-3
By Kingpen

THE ULTIMATE SACRIFICE 1-6
KHADIFI
IF YOU CROSS ME ONCE 1-3
ANGEL 1-4
IN THE BLINK OF AN EYE
By Anthony Fields

THE LIFE OF A HOOD STAR
By Ca$h & Rashia Wilson

NIGHTMARES OF A HUSTLA 1-3
BLOOD AND GAMES 1&2
By King Dream

GHOST MOB
By Stilloan Robinson

HARD AND RUTHLESS 1&2
MOB TOWN 251
THE BILLIONAIRE BENTLEYS 1-3
REAL G'S MOVE IN SILENCE
By Von Diesel

MOB TIES 1-7
SOUL OF A HUSTLER, HEART OF A KILLER 1-3
GORILLAZ IN THE TRENCHES
By SayNoMore

BODYMORE MURDERLAND 1-3
THE BIRTH OF A GANGSTER 1-4
By Delmont Player

FOR THE LOVE OF A BOSS 1&2
By C. D. Blue

KILLA KOUNTY 1-5
By Khufu

MOBBED UP 1-4
THE BRICK MAN 1-5
THE COCAINE PRINCESS 1-10

STEPPERS 1-3
SUPER GREMLIN 1-4
By King Rio

MONEY GAME 1&2
By Smoove Dolla

A GANGSTA'S KARMA 1-4
By FLAME

KING OF THE TRENCHES 1-3
By GHOST & TRANAY ADAMS

QUEEN OF THE ZOO 1&2
By Black Migo

GRIMEY WAYS 1-3
BETRAYAL OF A G
By Ray Vinci

XMAS WITH AN ATL SHOOTER
By Ca$h & Destiny Skai

KING KILLA 1&2
By Vincent "Vitto" Holloway

BETRAYAL OF A THUG 1&2
By Fre$h

THE MURDER QUEENS 1-5
By Michael Gallon

FOR THE LOVE OF BLOOD 1-4
By Jamel Mitchell

HOOD CONSIGLIERE 1&2
NO TIME FOR ERROR
By Keese

PROTÉGÉ OF A LEGEND 1&2
LOVE IN THE TRENCHES 1&2
By Corey Robinson

THE PLUG'S RUTHLESS DAUGHTER
By Tony Daniels

BORN IN THE GRAVE 1-3
CRIME PAYS
By Self Made Tay

MOAN IN MY MOUTH
By XTASY

TORN BETWEEN A GANGSTER AND A
GENTLEMAN
By J-BLUNT & Miss Kim

LOYALTY IS EVERYTHING 1-3
CITY OF SMOKE 1&2
By Molotti

HERE TODAY GONE TOMORROW 1&2
By Fly Rock

WOMEN LIE MEN LIE 1-4
FIFTY SHADES OF SNOW 1-3
STACK BEFORE YOU SPLURGE
GIRLS FALL LIKE DOMINOES
NAÏVE TO THE STREETS
By ROY MILLIGAN

PILLOW PRINCESS
By S. Hawkins

THE BUTTERFLY MAFIA 1-3
SALUTE MY SAVAGERY 1&2
By Fumiya Payne

THE LANE 1&2
By Ken-Ken Spence

THE PUSSY TRAP 1-5
By Nene Capri

DIRTY DNA
By Blaque

SANCTIFIED AND HORNY
by XTASY

# BOOKS BY LDP'S CEO, CA$H

TRUST IN NO MAN

TRUST IN NO MAN 2

TRUST IN NO MAN 3

BONDED BY BLOOD

SHORTY GOT A THUG

THUGS CRY

THUGS CRY 2

THUGS CRY 3

TRUST NO BITCH

TRUST NO BITCH 2

TRUST NO BITCH 3

TIL MY CASKET DROPS

RESTRAINING ORDER

RESTRAINING ORDER 2

IN LOVE WITH A CONVICT

LIFE OF A HOOD STAR

XMAS WITH AN ATL SHOOTER